The Amazing Adventures of

Sam the Bat

The Amazing Adventures of

Sam the Bat

Allyson Beatrice

Conservatory Press

San Francisco

Conservatory Press, an imprint of Plus One Press

Printed in the United States of America. For information, address Plus One Press, 2885 Golden Gate Avenue, San Francisco, California, 94118.

www.plusonepress.com

Book Design by Plus One Press

Cover and interior illustration of Sam by David Dorman
www.davedorman.com

ISBN-10: 0-9844362-1-9
ISBN-13: 978-0-9844362-1-7

2010933998

First Edition: November, 2010

10 9 8 7 6 5 4 3

For Gavin and Neave

Acknowledgements

A bucket full of gratitude to the following people for their support and guidance:

Ashley Avina, Rick Avina, Peter S. Beagle, Sam & Nina Beizai, Jacqui Biscobing, The Buffistas, Paula Carlson, Sean Carroll, Barbara Ferrer, Robin Fogelson, Dr. Sarah N. Gatson, Deborah Grabien, Nic Grabien, Bruce Haines, The Isle of Wight Bat Hospital, Isaac Klipstein, Beverly Leoczko, Lute Maleki, Robert Malesko, Kate McKean, Tim Minear, Joanne Nakayama, Jennifer Ouellette, Dr. Christopher Quick, Kristen Reidel, Dr. Daniel Riskin, Julie Schoenfeld, Section 335, Aurore Sibois, Sylvie Waskiewicz, and Jacqueline Zahas.

The Amazing Adventures of

Sam the Bat

Allyson Beatrice

Chapter 1
Birthquake

At 3:26am on April 17th, a young Mexican Free-Tail bat was born. His name was Sam.

The moon was full and round in the sky that night; it looked like a balloon filled with whipped cream, one breath from bursting. Sam began his life with a deep yawn, sucking the night air into his tiny lungs, soaking up a bit of that unusually enormous spring moon. Sam was so new that the effort of taking that first yawn was too much for him, and he closed his eyes, exhausted. Wrapped in his mother's leathery wings and cradled against her warm belly, he had a good, long rest. There was no way Sam could have known it, but this was the last time he would find himself sleepy or asleep at 3:26am for the rest of his life.

The night he was born, Sam was only one inch long, and weighed no more than a marshmallow. Together, Sam and his mother lived a contented life in a warm, tar-black cave in the Southern California desert. He lived with about eighty-four thousand, six hundred and ninety-two assorted relatives and friends, the cave like a bat city of chatter and laughter and the daily commutes of all those wings bursting in and out of the cave with the sun's settings and risings.

Every morning, as the earth spun lazily on its axis toward daylight, and the sky went from black to navy blue, Sam's mother would tell him a bedtime story. Each tale was about a cousin, auntie, or great-great-great-grampa's amazing bat adventures.

Sam's family had lived in this cave since bats could fly, and Sam's mother knew every story there was to tell about them.

"One night, long ago, Cousin Edith strayed too far from home and decided to spend the day in the old farmhouse past the ironwood trees. She found a quiet corner to spend the day, and had just closed her eyes to sleep when she heard a loud THWACK against the wall. She was so frightened that she lost her footing and swirled like a feather toward the hardwood floor. She spread her wings just before the business end of a straw broom would have given her a sound squashing. She spent half the morning diving and ducking from the farmer's wife. People are terribly inhospitable and downright rude to bats."

"What happened to Cousin Edith, mama? " Sam clung to his mother's belly even more tightly. She felt safe, and warm. "Did the Broom Wife kill her?"

Sam's mother chuckled softly. "You have to remember, Sam, if you find a way into a place, there must be a way out. Cousin Edith flew in through a hole in the screen door. Once she collected herself, she remembered the screen door. She flew back out and didn't stop beating her wings until she reached the cave."

Sam was quiet, thinking about the story. It didn't really make sense to him. He already knew about all sorts of predators that would like to eat him or his mother. But people didn't eat bats. Why would you try to squash something you didn't plan to eat?

"Why do people hate bats, mama?"

"Well, you have to feel a bit sorry for them, Sam. They can't fly. They're like snakes, stuck to the dirt and crawling on their bellies to pick their food out of the earth. But the thing about people is, they like to believe that they're the only animals that matter. They like to eat vegetables, and work very hard to tend to their crops. Moths love to eat the sweet leaves of the lettuces and tomato vines that people plant, and that makes people angry, because people don't like to share. You'd think people would be grateful to us for all the moths we eat, but they can't seem to tell the difference between bats and bugs. Perhaps they don't see very well, either."

Sam snuggled closer inside his mother's wings.

He was drowsy, and his eyes felt heavy. She shifted her claws and wriggled him awake.

"Before you sleep, little one, there's something I want you to remember. Where there are people, there will be food. If you're ever lost and hungry, listen for people. They're everywhere. Stay a safe distance from them, because they can be awfully cruel to bats, but wherever there are people, there are bugs. Follow the people, and dinner won't be far behind."

"Where there are people, there is food. I'll remember." Sam yawned. "G'night, Mama."

By the time he learned about how his Great-Great-Great Grampa Ricardo avoided becoming lunch to a hungry owl by steering a swarm of locusts right into the beast's path, Sam was too big for his mother to hold through the day. The night he learned that Auntie Enid, Uncle Ethan, and Cousin Eamon all met a terrible demise when each didn't notice a tomcat sneaking up behind them until he was in mid-pounce, Sam was strong enough to flutter about the cave on his own.

Sam's favorite story was a tale of adventure and mystery that had become legend in the cave amongst all the baby bats. As Sam's mother told it, long ago, a horrible drought had turned all the surrounding farmland into dust, and food had become scarce. The roost was slowly starving, and having to fly further and further in search of moths, mosquitoes, any bug at all to fill their bellies.

As the summer wore on, fewer bats were returning each night from the hunt, exhausting themselves before they could make the journey home before daybreak. Mothers struggled to feed their babies. The colony had never seen such desperate times.

"We had two choices, Sam: Starve, or separate. Those without babies to feed sacrificed the only home they had ever known, and set out to find a new cave. They gathered together in a flock so thick they blotted out the night sky. Instead of heading north toward the farms, they flew east, toward an unknown future."

Sam's eyes widened. He opened his mouth to

ask the half dozen questions swirling around in his head, but his mother continued before he could draw breath to speak.

"With only half the mouths to feed, we survived, but no one felt much like celebrating. Cousins, grandparents, and siblings had disappeared into the night, and they were missed. Everyone feared the worst, until a small search party of five bats returned to the cave just before the winter crept down from the north, with news of our lost family."

Sam's mother paused, getting sleepy, but Sam would have none of it. "Finish the story, mama! Where did the bats go? Were they eaten by cats? Or owls? Or cats with wings like owls?"

She laughed and kissed Sam's nose. "Well, as it turned out, they did find a new home, far, far away. But it wasn't a cave at all. One morning, desperate for rest before the sun rose, the colony had no choice but to roost under a bridge. Water rushed by below them, and the footsteps of people thundered above. That first day was a little scary, but when they woke to hunt the following evening, they found themselves in the center of a land rich with moths and mosquitoes. They ate so much they thought their bellies would burst. They came to like watching the boats sail by beneath them, and the breeze from the river. And that being close to the water meant they would never have to suffer drought, ever again."

Sam imagined a cool wind from the river teasing his ears and the scent of tall grasses filling his nose. He shivered a bit and nuzzled deeper against his mama's chest, warmed both by her and by the musky, spicy smell of the bats deep in the hot cave.

"Are they still there, mama?"

"As far as I know, they are. My mother always told me she was happy to know she had relatives far away, and that sometimes, when she was just a baby, she dreamed of visiting 'It sounds so glamorous,' she would say, 'living over a river, falling asleep with the sound of the water rushing by.' But I love our cave, Sam. Still, whenever someone doesn't return from the hunt, the older bats like to say that they went to live under the bridge."

Sam was quiet. He tried to imagine what it

would be like, roosting under a bridge, feeling that fuzzy, drowsy sensation come over him while the river rushed by, counting the leaves floating past, but he was asleep before he could get to three...

Every night, Sam's mother went out to hunt with the other grownup bats, and every morning returned with a full belly, listening for Sam's own special little song so she could find him in the dark of the cave. Sam would have his supper and she would begin a new story about his vast and colorful family. As the time grew near when he would have to fly and hunt for himself, Sam often wondered what his own life story would be like, and if it would involve a tomcat, a river, or an owl.

The first time he left the cave to hunt on his own, he carried his mother's stories with him. He always kept a watchful eye for owls and other beasts while munching on crispy, fluffy, delicious moths, which are like powdered jelly doughnuts if you happen to be a bat.

But it wasn't an owl, or a cat, or even an old woman armed with a broom that would change the course of Sam's life. A tiny burp that had begun deep in the belly of the earth would send Sam on a quest that would become the most requested bedtime story by baby bats around the world, from the agave fields of Mexico to the eucalyptus trees of Australia.

Early in the morning, as the first birds were singing to greet the sun, the bats were on their way home to their cave, their bellies full of crunchy, juicy bugs. Sam, however, wanted one last bite before darting back into the cave. His ears felt hot as the morning light struck his back. He found himself fixed on the fluttering wings of a moth in the distance between a brambly bush and his home, and darted toward the last nibble of the hunt.

CRUNCH!!!!

As he happily munched away in the last minutes of early dawn the sky suddenly went dark, and the air went still. Sam swallowed hard and looked up. What he mistook for a black cloud blotting out the morning sun was actually a thousand birds swirling upward like a tornado.

And then the rumbling began. The earth pitched upwards, sending Sam tumbling through the dirt. Stones jumped up from the ground like jackrabbits. As Sam spun across the desert like a tumbleweed in the wind, he could hear the crash as the mouth of the cave disappeared under a solid pile of rock. A wall of dust and debris roared toward him, knocking him backward into the brambly bushes. Sam's head snapped backward against a branch, knocking him unconscious.

It was almost dusk when Sam awoke. His brain felt like it was spinning inside his skull, and that last, fateful moth churned in his stomach. His wings were caught in the brambles, and he struggled to free himself. Exhausted, confused, and sore, he made his way back to the cave and his family.

The cave was gone.

Sloping down into the earth where his home had once stood, was a pile of rubble and tree limbs. Where there was once the din of chirping baby bats and the flapping of thousands of wings as his family groomed each other and dreamed in the dark safety of their home, there was now only silence.

Sam flew and clicked and sang until the sun sank into darkness, desperately listening for signs of life within the cave, but there was nothing but silence. A Joshua tree had fallen and landed roots-side-up where the mouth of the cave should have been. From above, it looked as if there had never been a cave at all. It had filled in with rock, making the hill one solid mass. As darkness fell over Southern California, Sam crumpled to the ground and cried. He'd never been alone before, never spent a day away from his mother and his family. And now they were all gone, buried under tons of rock, never to fly under the desert moon again.

He wept for his mother, for his cousins and aunties and all of his friends. In his grief, he didn't notice the owl closing in upon him until he felt the fur on the back of his neck stand up in fear. He turned and saw the razor-like talons inches away from clutching him up in their razor tips. He closed his eyes, took a deep breath, and waited to meet his doom.

Chapter 2
I've Got Bonnie

WHOOSH! CLACK!

Sam was snatched from the earth just before he heard the snap of a snake's jaws. It had been reaching for Sam in mid-spring before it belly-flopped in the dust where Sam had been standing only seconds before.

Sam understood what had happened. He knew

he was caught in the talons of a barn owl, and he had no fight left in him. He hung limply, tears rolling down his face, watching the gravesite that had been home to him and his family get smaller and further away as he was carried higher and higher into the air.

The owl flew through the trees and over a highway, further from Sam's hunting grounds than he'd ever been. It soared toward a broken-down cabin in the distance, letting out an ear-splitting screech that made Sam cry out in pain.

In the darkness, he heard the scurrying of dozens of small animals and birds clearing out of the cabin in fear. His captor glided through the window and lit down on a rafter, gingerly setting Sam on a soft bed of leaves and feathers.

Sam curled under his wings. "Will it hurt?"

The owl bent down to Sam. "Will what hurt?" she whispered.

Sam's voice was muffled by his wings. "Being eaten."

"I'm not going to eat you, baby. I don't think I want to eat ever again." The owl's voice, much like

Sam's, sounded sad and numb. "That was your cave, wasn't it? The one that was buried?"

For the first time, Sam peeked out from under his wings and looked at the owl. She was a barn owl, her face pale and heart-shaped, and her eyes big black pools reflecting light. For a moment, Sam thought he could see the whole night sky in them.

Sam's eyes welled up again. This was his enemy, the awful thing that hunted bats like him, like his mother, like his family, but he was too overwhelmed with sadness to be afraid.

"My mama, my family... they're all gone."

The words caught in Sam's throat. He hoped the universe wouldn't hear him, or maybe that it would show him he was wrong. Maybe it would change its mind, turn back time and start the day over. Then he could warn his family, bring them back, let them all be together again, warm in their cave.

"I'm all alone."

"No." The owl said, her voice a low rasp. "You're not alone."

With that, she scooped Sam up and set him to roost upside-down on the rafter above her. She snapped up a moth that was fluttering in the moonlight and offered it to Sam.

He met the owl's beak with his own fanged mouth, and gulped down the moth in one bite. It was almost a kiss, and Sam felt the tiniest pebble of comfort deep in his belly.

"My name is Bonnie, and I won't leave you." She stroked his face with the edge of her wing and then nuzzled him gently. Her face felt soft and warm, like his mother's. "I'll keep you safe, baby."

Early next evening, as Sam was struggling to shake off the last moments of a bad dream, Bonnie stirred in her nest and cleared her throat.

"We had five children," she began. "I was tending to the eggs, and Nathan—Nathan is—was - " Her voice cracked. "Nathan was my life-mate. He was coming home late each night because he was hunting for both of us. It was just dawn when he returned with supper, and then..." Bonnie stopped.

Sam finished the sentence for her. "And then the earth shook."

"The rafter collapsed from under me, and our nest, our children... our babies..." Bonnie swallowed the lump in her throat. "Nathan dove down into the straw, trying to find our eggs, and that's when the earth heaved up one last time, and the walls came down. I don't know how I wasn't crushed. I don't know why I survived. I wish I hadn't. My heart is underneath all of that wood, back there in that old barn."

"I flew and flew until I thought my lungs would burst. When I couldn't beat my wings anymore, I set down on that branch near your cave, Sam. When I saw you, I knew that we were the same. I heard your cry, and I knew. Then I saw the snake."

"And you saved me," Sam whispered. He looked up at Bonnie, leaning in toward those big, dark eyes. Bonnie raised her wing and pulled Sam close to her face.

"I saved someone's baby."

Sam and Bonnie stayed in their cabin for three nights, Bonnie catching mice that scuttled past on the floor, and Sam catching moths that wandered into the rafters on moonbeams. On the fourth night, just a moment before a thumbnail of moon pierced the sky, Bonnie rustled her feathers.

"Time to fly, little one."

"Where will we go, Bonnie?"

"Come here to me, Sam." Bonnie held him. Her warmth up against him, the sound of her voice, reminded him achingly of his mama, holding him tight in their roost and telling him a bedtime story.

"Long ago, in a faraway land called Argentina, before I was even an egg in a nest, there was an owl named Nina." Bonnie's voice was strong and deep.

"There wasn't a hawk that could touch her, she was so fast. Everyone said she was the most graceful hunter in the sky. She was clever, beautiful, and she had a laugh that could make even the angriest hornet smile. Her wings were a rich golden caramel and her face was the creamiest white you ever saw. Some say she was the loveliest Barn Owl who ever lived."

Looking up at Bonnie, Sam thought she could very well be describing herself, but he stayed quiet. Bonnie nuzzled him, and went on with her story.

"Nina was courted by every male Barn Owl in Argentina. But she fell in love with a funny little owl from Texas, named Clementé. Clementé was a terrible clown. He entertained her with silly love poems, and often pretended that the rats he caught were actually eating him. Nina's papa thought Clementé was a fool, and did his best to discourage them from seeing each other. But young love burns brighter than the noonday sun, so Nina and Clementé eloped and traveled all the way up to these woods to start their family."

"Nina was your mother, wasn't she?" Sam asked, already knowing he was right.

"How did you guess?"

Sam smiled. He wanted to tell her that she was just as lovely, maybe even lovelier than the way she described her mama. But his cheeks warmed with shy embarrassment.

"You sound just like me, when I talk about my mama."

"My mother told me all about Argentina. It's a lush forest full of life. It's not dry and dusty at all. The air smells like flowers and earth and ocean. And there are bats there, Sam. Just like you. Thousands of them, blacking out the moon and all the stars when they burst out from their homes. That's where we'll go, Sam. I'm taking you there."

Sam filled his whole chest with a deep breath of the night air. "How do we get there?"

"We fly south until all we can see is ocean, to the very end of the earth itself," Bonnie's eyes twinkled under the starlight. "These woods, this desert... we can't stay here, Sam. The memories of what we've lost are crushing us with sadness. We need to find a new home. Together. Are you ready to fly? Sam, what is it? What's wrong?"

Sam's eyes had gone wide. "Bonnie, my mama told me that long ago, some of my family moved to a bridge over a river! But it was to the east. Maybe they're still there!"

"Well then, we'll travel southeast. We'll check under every bridge on the way. If we don't find them, you're safe with me until we get to Argentina."

Sam grinned. He felt the spirit of his entire colony lifting him up. He and Bonnie swooped out through the broken window together, cutting a path through the darkness.

It took Sam and Bonnie one hundred and sixty-two days to travel the six thousand miles to Argentina.

Sam would climb as high as he could into the sky, trying his hardest to reach the moon. Then he'd catch the wind, speeding forward into the night. He'd circle back for Bonnie, who hovered close to the ground to catch mice. She was a graceful hunter, but she was slower than Sam, who could feed on swarms of insects while zipping along on the breeze.

Bonnie kept a sharp ear trained on Sam, listening for any sign of a threat. Sometimes she would carry him in her talons, to keep him safe from other owls. Whenever a predator got too close, she'd scoop Sam up as if she were going to take a tasty treat back to her nest. Safe under Bonnie's wings, Sam would close his eyes and feel the wind on his face, listening to the changing sounds of nature, as they traveled further south toward the rainforests. His nose filled with the scent of a moist, heavy earth and the sticky sweet smell of berries and nectarines growing in the rich soil. It was a lovely way to fly.

They slept wherever they could find shelter. Sometimes they were fortunate enough to find a warm barn, but mostly they camped in rotted-out trees, where Bonnie would hide Sam away for the day, guarding him on a branch close by.

Every day, as the sun was rising, Sam told Bonnie bedtime stories of his own.

"There were thousands of bat pups, just like me." His mourning heart was made lighter by a sense of hope and Bonnie's companionship. "No one but our mothers were allowed into the nursery, with a few males standing guard outside to keep us safe."

Bonnie leaned closer to Sam, not wanting to miss a single word. "How did your mama find you when she came back from the hunt? Out of all those thousands of babies?"

"Every bat pup has his own special song. I knew my song the minute I was born, and sang it to my mama the first time she wrapped her wings around me to keep me warm. When she came back to the cave every morning, I would sing for her and she would know just where I was."

He often told her his favorite story, about the bats under the bridge. "I wonder if they're still there. I wonder if they tell each other stories about my cave."

"Perhaps we'll find them soon. I'm sure they would love to meet you."

"I'd love to meet them! And roost over the river! I bet they know who my Great-Great-Great Grampa Ricardo was!"

"Well, Sam, I think we should ask every bat we meet along the way. I'm sure someone knows about your bridge and can tell us how to get there."

"And you can live with us!" Sam beamed with new purpose.

Bonnie managed a weak smile. It was unlikely

that an owl would be welcome in a bat colony. The best she could do for Sam was to help find him a new home, and to finish his mother's lessons on how to defend himself from predators. For the rest of their journey together, she taught him all she knew about evading a predator like herself.

He learned how to hiss like a snake, screech like an owl, and how to roll onto his back to claw, kick, and bite at an enemy, should he ever be cornered. He learned to keep clear of open fields where a silent owl could hear him click and could swoop in to gobble him up so quickly that he'd be inside its belly before he even knew he was eaten.

Sam had no idea he was learning how to think like an owl, how to defend himself like an owl. He just knew that Bonnie was very proud of him when he could hunt and fly in silence, gliding on the wind like a leaf, especially when he could zip out ahead of her, undetected for miles.

All the while, they searched beneath every bridge and overpass, whether or not there was a river running under it. They mostly found nothing, but sometimes they'd surprise one or two roosting bats who would be frightened away at the sight of Bonnie before Sam could even ask if they had heard of his ancestral river colony.

Just as they were about to cross the border from Paraguay into Argentina, Bonnie called to Sam to slow down and come back to nest in an abandoned shack for the day. It was a bit early to stop, but one look at Bonnie's face told Sam that she had something important to say.

"Sam," Bonnie began. "I couldn't be more proud of you if you were one of my own chicks. But, I think it's time we found some bats for you to play with. I've taught you everything I know about being an owl, but only a bat can teach you what it is to be a bat."

Sam was bewildered. "I haven't spoken to one single bat since we left the cabin."

Bonnie's voice was very gentle. "They're frightened of me, Sam. And they should be. Owls... owls eat bats. Most owls, anyway. I ate bats before I met you, Sam."

What Bonnie didn't say was that she would never eat another bat. Neither would her children, or her children's children. Bonnie would forbid it for as long as she lived, and owls live for a long, long time.

"When we cross the border, we'll find a colony for you to join, so that you can roost and hunt. Maybe someday you'll fall in love and have children of your own."

Sam wrinkled his nose again. "Ewwwwww!!!!! I'm not going to fall in love, Bonnie! Girls smell like a lizard's butt!"

"Well, even so, Sam, you're the smartest, strongest bat I've ever met, and I'm very sure that there's a bat nursery that could use a Guard Bat like you to protect them."

Sam puffed out his chest, remembering how he'd loved and looked up to the heroic males who had guarded his family's nursery. But then he remembered Bonnie, and deflated.

"But where will you live, Bonnie? In the cave, with me? Maybe if we talk to the other bats, they'll know you won't eat them, and they won't be afraid of you!"

Even as he said it, Sam knew Bonnie could

never live in a colony. She needed lots of room to move and spread her wings. She needed the quiet. Sam, being a true bat just as she was a true owl, needed everything she didn't. He missed being part of a colony, thousands of cousins chirping and flapping as one, exploding out of the cave for the evening's hunt. He missed the happy-hungry songs of bat pups greeting their mothers at the end of night.

"Will you be okay by yourself, Bonnie?"

"I will miss you every day for the rest of my days." Bonnie's voice was steady, but she ached. She loved Sam from the tips of her talons to the polka-dots on her feathers. She reached out to cuddle him close, the way she had the night they met. "Tomorrow, we'll set out early to find you a colony and a cave."

Sam snuggled against Bonnie's heart-shaped face. What neither of them knew was that, hidden behind a broom on the southwest corner of the shack, were four eyes fixed on them, and two fanged mouths hanging open in the shape of capital "O"s.

The two vampire bats had been feasting on a

sleeping rat as big as a coyote in a dark corner of the shack when they witnessed the most amazing sight of their lives; a bat with an owl for a pet.

Vampire bats are terrible gossips. By the time Sam and Bonnie woke, word had spread throughout the rainforest, and nearly every creature from miles around had gathered to see the unlikely pair emerge from the shack.

Chapter 3
Batcula

When Sam slept, his breath and heartbeat slowed like a hibernating bear's. In this drowsy twilight, his dreams about his mother, his home, and hunting were so vivid that the musky sweet smell of the cave tickled his nose, and he could taste the powdery sweetness of a moth in his mouth. In some dreams, his home wasn't a cave, but a perch above a river, and he didn't cross a desert to hunt, but a stretch of tall grasses that led to rich farmlands.

As Sam spread his wings and caught a tailwind in his dream, he also stretched them while he hung from his roost. He opened his eyes slowly. The dream sank away and Bonnie's figure came into focus. She was perched near a splintery hole in the wall of the shack, frozen like a statue, staring out into the jungle.

Sam listened, hoping to hear whatever it was that Bonnie was seeing. He could hear birds settling into nests. Closer, he heard the wind in the trees, rustling the tender ferns that surrounded them. He could smell the rich black soil, flowers, and the heavy, musky, sweet scent of animals... lots of them.

The little shack was deep in the jungle, far from farmland or livestock, but he was suddenly sure they had lost their bearings and ended up surrounded by a herd of goats and cattle.

Sam couldn't have guessed what Bonnie saw, because no animal, living or dead, had ever seen anything so wondrous. Staring back at them were a thousand eyes, wide with curiosity. There was a herd of capybaras, the giant rats of the jungle. Toucans and parrots hung on every tree branch like Christmas ornaments. Pumas and jaguars crouched beside raccoons and pig-like peccaries. It should have been a great feast outside, hungry predators and easy prey. But no one hunted. No one was eating, and no one was getting eaten. There was a strange truce in the jungle. Whatever they were waiting for must be far more interesting than dinner.

Bonnie scanned the snouts and beaks in the crowd for a hint of why all these animals had gathered around the shack. And then she saw them: A little group of vampire bats clinging to a rotten log, huddled together, staring with unblinking eyes and beaming their cheerful little grins. Terrible gossips.

Sam had moved up behind Bonnie's shoulder. "Did you find a colony?"

"SHHHHHHH!!!!!" Bonnie clapped her wing over Sam's face. "Yes, I did. But these bats are tricky little fellows, and we're going to have to do something special to impress them. We're going to play a game, and I need you to listen very carefully. We are going to fly and I want you to follow me and do everything I do."

Dark had crept through the rainforest, and all those staring eyes glowed yellow under a full moon. The wind died down, and the crowd held its breath.

"EEEEAHHHHHHEEEEEEEE!!!!!!" Bonnie shot out of the shack like a cannonball. Sam followed, close on her tail, echoing her every dive and twist just as she had instructed him. He glided under her, she reached for him with her talons, and he caught hold and flipped upside down, an acrobat hanging from a living trapeze with no net. Wrapping his wings around himself as if he were napping, Sam giggled happily as Bonnie hovered above the crowd. Startled by their gasp, he let go and started to flutter toward the earth below.

Bonnie swooped under him and caught him on her back before he hit the ground. Sam peeked out from her speckled wing, and saw that every jaw and beak had dropped open, staring in amazement at the owl and the bat dancing in the moonlight.

The colony of vampire bats started to cheer. Sam beamed down at them, thrilled at the sight of other bats, even as funny looking as they were. Where Sam was clumsy on two feet, they crept easily along the rotting log on their elbows and feet. Their grinning faces were very different from Sam's, from their pointy ears to their diamond-shaped snouts to their fanged mouths.

Nevertheless, these were bats. They had wings and fur and they chirped cheerily. Sam swelled with hope, and forgot that he was riding the wind with Bonnie until she circled down and landed on the ground in front of the log. She stood straight and tall, and then took a deep bow in front of the colony, which honored the pair with wild applause.

Sam tumbled off her back into the moss, stunned by the hoopla.

"I'll stay close for awhile, baby. These bats will take care of you now, and you'll be safe." Bonnie nuzzled Sam's face against her beak. "Someday, I hope I have a dozen chicks, just as wonderful as you are."

With that, she launched herself into the air, not

looking back as she sailed into the jungle. She didn't want Sam to see the tears welling in her eyes.

"Showtime's over..." a jaguar purrrrrrred. He dropped to a crouch, ready to pounce.

The jungle burst into chaos. With no encore performance of the Sam and Bonnie Show, everyone resumed their natural roles of Those Who Eat and Those Who Are Eaten. There was a sudden, explosive stampede as deer and pigs dove into the ferns to escape the terrifying jaws of the big cats.

The vampire bats flapped their wings at Sam. "C'mon!" one of them squealed. "We have to go! Come with us! Hurry! RUN!!!!!"

Sam tried to follow as the vampire bats hopped off the log and actually ran across the forest floor. Sam stumbled and fell and panted, trying to keep up with them. The vampire bats galloped like horses through the brush in a herd, with Sam lagging behind. He wasn't made for ground travel.

"Hey! Guys!" Sam stumbled and choked. "Guys! Wait! Wait for me! Why don't you just FLY?" Sam stumbled again, caught his breath, and took flight. He glided low, just above them.

"Hey! You! Why don't you just RUN???" one of the bats hollered at Sam.

Despite the differences in self-transportation, the group stayed together. They charged into the opening of an abandoned mine, long forgotten by those who built it... and those who built it long forgotten by everyone else.

Safe inside the mine, Sam's new friends burst into howling laughter, congratulating each other in clicks and chirps in their strange musical accents for the quick getaway.

Sam listened to them chirping the story of his moonlit dance with Bonnie. They were far more animated than his colony, gesturing wildly with their wings and acting out the night's events as they described them. More bats appeared from deeper within the mine, laughing and chirping approval. Listening to the echoes bouncing off the walls, Sam could tell it was a tiny colony of maybe seventy or so from the sounds of their beating wings and the chirps. The activity in Sam's desert cave seemed deafening in comparison. From the way the echoes bounced into his ears in a muffled ring, the mine seemed to go very deep into the earth, but the colony appeared to prefer roosting closer to the opening.

And then all was quiet, as everyone turned toward Sam and waited for him to speak.

"I... I don't know what to say."

A female bat, about the same age as his mother before the earthquake took her, waved him toward her perch, coaxing him with an outstretched wing. Sam flew up to her, and she cuddled him close. He was too big for her to carry, so he just snuggled deep into her chest from his perch next to her. She bit her tongue and offered her blood to Sam.

He was horrified. Looking around, he saw that all over the mine, young bats were lapping up blood off bigger ones. Sam couldn't bring himself to taste it, though he had only caught a few mosquitoes that had crossed his path on the run back to the mine and his belly was empty. He turned his head away from the wound.

Sam couldn't understand why the bats were eating each other's blood, or why they weren't out hunting in the middle of the night. All through the night he listened to them chatter on, feeling lost and hoping that Bonnie had kept her word about staying close to make sure he was all right. He needed to find another colony, one that liked bugs, not blood.

Eventually, a bit of light spilled into the cave. Sam fell asleep wrapped in the wings of a stranger, dreaming of his mother and the legendary bridge over the river.

Sam woke early the next evening, because he was so used to flying on Bonnie's schedule. The brood was silent and sleeping as the last shards of sunlight cut patterns across the floor near the opening of the mine. He yawned and stretched... and tumbled out of the wings of the bat who had been holding him, and landed right into a puddle of guano.

"Ewwwwwwwwwwww!!!!!!!!" cried Sam.

As he staggered out of the smelly goo and collected himself, he was bowled over by a husky, scrappy bat, baring his fangs and stuffing the surprised Sam's mouth with a pebble to stifle a scream. He wasn't a vampire bat, or a Mexican free-tail. His ears were rounded and his fur a mottled brown.

"I don't know who you are," the stranger hissed, "but I've worked TOO HARD and TOO LONG to watch some pipsqueak like you ruin my plans with The Dark Lord!"

Then the bat froze, his face a crazy, twisted frown. He sniffed. "Why do you stink of poo?" he asked, and dropped Sam like a stone.

"RENNY!" A voice boomed from overhead.

The scrappy bat grabbed Sam by the throat, hid him and grinned. "Maaaaahster," cooed Renny. "How may I be of service to you this evening? Look! I've brought you a delicious victim!" Renny bowed and then nodded toward the entrance.

A sleeping pig, snoring like a band saw around a shiny red apple stuffed in its mouth, was sprawled at the opening of the mine. It was completely ridiculous that a bat could have managed this display, but there it was.

Suddenly, out of the darkness slipped an elderly bat, older than any Sam had ever seen. As he moved into the moonlight, the old one curled his gray ears back against his head and grabbed a red ceibo petal to drape around him like a cape. His shadow loomed freakishly large behind him.

"What are you hiding there, Renny?" the old one demanded.

"What? This?" Renny pulled Sam out from behind his back. "I was just tidying him up a bit!" Renny beat Sam against the ground like a rug, a cloud of dried bat poop puffing up all around them.

The old bat stood straight and tall, raised his chin and pointed toward Renny with a paper-thin wrinkled wing. "This little bat is our guest, Renny. He's traveled very far to get here, and he's tired and hungry. You are to show him some hospitality and bring him some of those repulsive moths you're always stuffing in your mouth."

Renny's jaw dropped, obviously wounded. But he offered his best shot at a genuine, toothy grin, and bowed deeply.

"I will do your bidding gladly, Maaaahster." Renny turned to leave and sneered at Sam, his batty fists balled in anger. The ancient bat watched Renny fly out into the night. Then he grinned warmly, and introduced himself.

"My name is Papa Ernesto, little one. This is my family, and my home. I heard the wonderful story about you and the owl last night. You're a very brave little bat. I'm sorry I didn't introduce myself earlier, but I'm very old and very tired, and all the excitement was too much for me."

"My name is Sam, and I'm so happy to meet you, Papa Ernesto. I've been looking for a colony for a very long time."

Sam told his story: his mama, the earthquake, Bonnie, and the legendary bridge over the river that sheltered his long lost cousins. When he finished, he looked toward Papa Ernesto and cocked his head, which was heavy with questions about this new colony.

"Why don't you fly? Why is your family so small? Why do you eat blood? Why are you wearing a flower petal? Why did that weird little bat try to kill me?"

Papa Ernesto laughed, and took Sam's wings in his claws. "Hush little one, I'll answer all of your questions."

He explained that some bats eat bugs, some like fruit and nectar, but that vampire bats, like his family, feed on the blood of animals. "You eat moths. Do they not have blood in their veins?"

Sam had no answer; he'd never thought about it that way before. Papa Ernesto explained that vampire bats learned long ago to stay close to the ground and run fast, so that they could hunt snakes and other small mammals.

"Cattle are easy. They fall asleep and we can sneak up and take a taste from a leg, just above the hoof," he said, raising one winged claw to neck height.

"What about the mean little bat who tried to strangle me? Why did he call you the Daaaahk Loooord?"

"Ah, Renny," Papa Ernesto said, shaking his head. "His is a sad story. Renny arrived eleven full moons ago from a faraway land across the sea called England. Sounds like a terrible place. Cold and rainy all the time. Dirty. Too many people. People are such filthy creatures..."

Sam gently pushed the old bat back on course. "So what about Renny?"

"Ah! Renny. He told me a fantastic story about a vampire bat called 'Dracula.' The Dracula bat eats blood like we do. It must be magic blood, because he never grows any older and never dies. He wears a big cape and has poofy hair on his head. Renny said the whole world fears and respects this bat, but we had never heard of him. I think Renny is just a bit crazy for believing such a fairy tale."

Sam nodded. Renny seemed more than just a bit crazy.

"I wrap a petal around me when I am cold, and so Renny mistook me for this Dracula fellow, thinking that since I eat blood and wear a cape, I must be him. Renny thinks if I let him drink my blood, he'll live forever and be feared and respected. It's terribly silly."

"Why don't you tell Renny the truth? Why do you let him make a fool of himself?"

Papa Ernesto pointed his wing toward the snoring pig, and Sam saw six happy little bats cheerfully licking a pool of blood from its rump. They all waved at Sam.

"He offered to be my personal servant for as long as I want, if I promised to someday let him drink my blood. I of course told him that the whole idea was ridiculous, but he keeps bringing food for the colony, perhaps hoping I will change my mind."

Sam's shoulders dropped in sadness. It seemed wrong of them to take advantage of Renny, even if he was mean and crazy.

Though Papa Ernesto was old, he was not blind. He saw that Sam didn't approve of how they were treating the scrappy, crazy bat, and hurried to explain.

"It may seem that we are taking advantage of the poor mad fellow. But you must understand that before Renny came here, there were only two dozen of us. We were hunted by people who thought we were making their cattle sick, and by -" he coughed. "By, well, owls."

"Bonnie doesn't eat bats!"

"No, but not all owls are like your Bonnie, little one. In fact, I think she's the only owl in all the

45

world who wouldn't snap up a bat for dinner in a heartbeat."

Sam couldn't disagree with him on that point.

"As for Renny, I have never promised him anything. What harm is there in benefiting from his foolish beliefs?" Papa Ernesto didn't seem to really want an answer. "The truth is that Renny keeps us safe, Sam. Our family has doubled in size, and we haven't lost one bat to predators. We never have to leave the mine. Renny brings us dinner, and we stay in all night and tell stories. We're happy, we have no worries... except that every now and again the young ones sneak out to hunt. And then we worry all night about them. Young bats forget that the world can be a very dangerous place; they think they'll live forever, like in Renny's silly stories. I do my best to keep an eye on them, to keep them safe."

Sam opened his mouth to reply, but just then, Renny returned. He was steering a large swarm of fireflies followed by a fluttering cloud of moths into the mouth of the cave. Sam's jaw dropped in wonder. Dinner had arrived.

"Besides, where else would a crazy bat like

Renny live?" Papa Ernesto whispered. "We let him stay with us, he amuses us with his fairytales, everyone is happy."

But Renny didn't look happy. He looked exhausted, and mad as a hornet.

Sam ate, but his supper tasted like sand in his mouth. He hadn't earned his meal. Restless, he fluttered to the opening of the mine to peek outside at the jungle, and breathe fresh air. His ears caught the sound of wings flapping, and out of the corner of his eye he saw a pale face peering through the trees like a ghost. It was Bonnie.

Sam chirped happily and waved a wing, but she was gone as quickly as she had appeared.

"Sam..." Papa Ernesto called. "Stay close to home."

Sam sighed and tried to hop back like the vampire bats did, but he just stumbled and tripped clumsily, like a broken brambly branch caught in a storm. He gave up and flew back inside the mine.

Sam tried to fit in, but even though they were bats like him, he couldn't help feeling out of place and different.

Papa Ernesto told scary stories to the pups every night, about how dangerous it was outside the mine. Bonnie had taught Sam to be careful, but never fearful. Further back, his mother's bedtime stories had never frightened him. She had always made the world outside sound so exciting and beautiful. Papa Ernesto made the world outside seem like a nightmare, with hungry jaws and sharp claws lurking around every corner. He wo uld act out stories of bats tricked and eaten by terrible monsters with red glowing eyes and dagger-like teeth, prowling in the moonlight. Papa Ernesto would stand with his back to the far wall of the mine, the moon casting a menacing shadow behind him. The pups would tremble in fear as he told stories of horror and death. He never spoke of the beauty of the moon and stars, or the sweet scent of fresh air against your face while gliding on a breeze.

And so it went, night after night. Renny would appear with a goat or a pig or a capybara, and a swarm of moths and mosquitoes for Sam. The colony was so fat they could barely hold on to their perches, and began sleeping on the ground in the daytime.

Sometimes, Sam would get as close to the mouth of the mine as he could, listening for Bonnie's call, or hoping to see a flash of her speckled wings. But there was nothing. He had always known that his time with Bonnie would end. He just hadn't wanted it to be so soon.

Sam was getting fatter as well. And he was terribly restless. The mine might be safe, but he missed the hunt, flapping his wings, catching a tailwind and zooming along, trying to catch the moon.

He longed for freedom, and resolved to speak to Papa Ernesto about his desire to fly, and perhaps search for the bridge he was dreaming of more and more often.

The next evening, Papa Ernesto listened carefully as Sam made his case about the moon, stars, wind, and how heavy his belly felt.

"You're welcome to stay with us as long as you

like, Sam, but these are my rules. They exist to keep us together, to make sure our pups have the opportunity to grow up and not risk being eaten."

Sam winced. "But Papa, my family was lost inside our home. I survived because I was outside, hunting." His voice got quieter; he didn't want to be disrespectful. "No place is safe forever."

Papa Ernesto couldn't argue with Sam on that point. But he also held a secret. He was too old to hunt. He could barely outrun a turtle. Renny's servitude had lengthened his life, his time with his family, and he wasn't ready to give that up. He didn't want Sam to complain any louder, and banishing him wasn't an option. Sam was a hero, a legend amongst his family because of his flight with the owl. Papa Ernesto had to compromise.

"Sam, you are very special. You survived an earthquake, and you charmed an owl to protect you. Because of this, I think you possess the strength to venture out of the mine. Hunt with Renny tomorrow. Tell him I said you will help him from now on."

The next evening, before the rest of the vampire

colony woke, Sam shyly approached Renny as he stretched and mumbled to himself, preparing to find another amazing dinner for the roost.

"Renny," Sam whispered.

Renny continued to mumble and preen himself, oblivious to Sam.

"Renny. Renny. RENNY!" Sam yelled.

"EEP!" Renny screamed, and Sam pressed a wing against Renny's mouth to shush him before he woke the sleeping colony.

"Renny. Papa Ernesto says I can help you tonight!"

"I don't NEED your help!"

"Please, Renny? I'm tired of staying inside all the time. I need to stretch my wings and fly with you. It must make you so tired to do this by yourself, and I can help. Look! I'm very strong!" Sam tried to lift the sleeping capybara, which had been last night's dinner, with no luck.

Renny furrowed his brow in anger. He had never liked Sam. He was sure that Papa Ernesto/Dracula was going to make Sam a vampire, even though he hadn't earned it.

"Please, Renny? Papa Ernesto won't let me go out alone... he said to tell you that I have to help you!" Sam pleaded.

And then a terrible, brilliant, horrible idea hit Renny. His frown turned up into a toothy, crazy grin. He ruffled the fur on Sam's head so hard that Sam almost fell over into the dirt.

"Of course you can come help me, little guy." The crooked crazy grin got wider, exposing Renny's bright, needle-sharp fangs.

He had finally thought of a way to get rid of Sam. Forever.

Chapter 4
Sam vs. Man

"Come with me, young Sam." Renny took Sam by the wing, and smiled. "I've always wanted to bring the Dark Lord a whale for dinner, but I just can't lift one by myself. I think that together, we can bring him the finest meal he's ever had."

"What's a whale?" Sam asked, fascinated.

"It's a creature that lives in the ocean, not far

from here. They swim all day, but sometimes they come up to breathe the air and look at the stars. Stupid creatures. They're like cows with no legs. We can catch one, you and I. Come. Let's get a whale."

Sam could hardly contain his excitement as they took off from the mine, but his overstuffed belly made it difficult to fly, and he huffed and puffed as he followed Renny through the jungle. "Wait! Wait for me!" Sam shouted.

Renny began to play a game with Sam. Over and over, he would disappear behind a tree, and Sam, struggling to keep up, would fly right past as Renny hid and giggled. He kept it up all the way to the docks, where the exhausted Sam finally dropped from the sky to rest on the railing of a ship.

"Come on, you lazy little bat!" said Renny. "Wait until I tell Papa Ernesto how slow you are. We're never going to get his dinner back in time now!"

Sam needed to rest. He hadn't flown in so long, and carrying his round belly made him even slower. He thought his heart would burst, but was determined to bring the whale back to the colony and prove that he was as strong and clever as Renny. Despite the pain and weariness, Sam followed Renny out to sea.

As they flew further and further from the shoreline, Sam's wings felt weaker than ever. He dipped low to the ocean, trying to glide along the wind and conserve energy. He could feel his heart pounding in his ears, and every muscle in his body ached.

"Renny. Renny. Please. I have to rest. We have to go back," Sam pleaded.

But Renny was already halfway back to the shore, laughing to himself.

"I hope you can swim, lazy little bat!" Renny called out.

Sam tried to turn back, but the wind was against him, and he struggled to stay above the waves. "Please Renny! Please come back!"

There was no response. A gust of wind pulled him further out to sea, where he saw a bright light shining out over the black water. He rode the wind toward the beacon, pumping his wings only when he dipped close enough to the water to feel the salty spray lick at his belly.

A ship came into focus, a huge vessel with a deck that seemed to stretch for miles. Sam found one last burst of strength somewhere deep in his gut, and launched himself at the deck. He skimmed along the deck, tumbling wings over feet until he came to a stop in a puddle of salt water. He dragged himself into a dark corner behind a staircase, found a rusty pipe on which to roost, and immediately fell into a deep sleep.

It was the fat stored in his belly from months of being fed by Renny that would keep him alive for the first few days on the ship. Without that, he would have surely died from hunger.

And had it not been for the colony of rats that had taken up residence below his roost, he might have died of loneliness.

He heard them before he saw them. His ears twitched, hearing the tinny scratches of claws on metal and the sweet squeaks of hungry mouths. When he opened his eyes, he saw a wriggling nest of what looked like wingless bats with chubby, squishy bellies jostling for attention from their mother. They were surrounded by big burlap sacks full of dried grains. Sam fell in and out of consciousness, unsure where his dreams of his colony stopped and the sounds of the happy family below began.

There was a mother rat with five hungry pups who seemed to nurse constantly. Their mama nibbled at a pile of grain that had pooled at her side through a gnawed hole in the burlap. He saw several others in the rat colony scurrying over the grain sacks.

Sam watched the rat pups play, chattering and

tumbling all over each other in a pile of soft bellies and fur, and a tangle of tails and whiskers. They were happy and warm, completely safe with their mama and their family. They napped, nursed, and wrestled together without fear or worry. Sam remembered feeling that content, back home in the roost with all the other pups, singing to his mother as she sailed through the ocean of chirping, wriggling bats to find him and hold him close. Sam felt homesick for a home that was no more, and watching the rats made him long for family. Out here, in the middle of the ocean, he was beginning to lose hope of ever finding the bridge over the river.

His belly rumbled and whined. He had no idea when his next meal would come from, or if the ship would ever reach land where he could hunt. The mama rat began to sing a lullaby to her pups, and Sam forgot his hunger for a moment, comforted by the memories of his own mama.

From the ends of your whiskers to the tips of your tails,
I love you like chimes love the breeze.
From the gleam in your eyes to the claws on your feet,

I love you like trees love their leaves.
From the wet of your nose to the soft of your fur,
I love you like the sea loves the shore.
From the beat of your heart to the snore in your sleep,
I love you forever and ever and more.

Sam's face was damp with tears as he hid in his roost, smiling down at the rat colony, falling asleep to their rhythmic snores and sighs. Just as he drifted into dream, Sam was jolted awake by a loud BOOM! that shook his roost and sent the rats squealing and scurrying in every direction. The pups froze in fear, backed into a corner behind their mother.

Before them, a human was staring the colony down through the sight of a long black pipe. His shoulders were tense, his sun-leathered face twisted in a sneer of disgust. His fingers pulled back on a curved bit of metal on the bottom of the pipe just as one of the larger male rats lunged at his leg, throwing him off balance. A spray of pellets blasted from the pipe and cut through the burlap sacks. Rivers of grain poured onto the floor.

The man shook the rat off his leg and kicked it hard, sending it mewling across the filthy floor, injured and stunned. The man took aim again.

Sam saw, but didn't understand. The man meant to launch the pellets right through the mother and pups, killing them. But why?

Rage boiled up from Sam's gut. He saw the man point the pellet gun toward the mother rat, but before he could grip the trigger, Sam attacked. Without any thought for his own safety, Sam pierced the air with a screech like Bonnie's warning cry.

"YOU LEAVE THEM ALONE!"

Sam's claws ripped at the long black curls that spilled down the man's face and neck. The man screamed, dropped his weapon, and began clawing at Sam, who bit the man's fingers and shouted at him through tears of rage.

"BULLY! FILTHY CREATURE! COWARD!!!" Sam took a final swipe at the man's face with a clawed foot, ripping a bloody wound on his cheek.

Sam pulled away, and the man ran screaming into the darkness of the ship's belly. Exhausted, Sam fluttered to the floor and wrapped his wings around his face. The smell of the man's sweat all over his wings made Sam want to retch, but his empty stomach had nothing to spill.

"Hello? Hello, little bat," a gentle voice called to Sam.

Sam peeked out over his wing. The mother rat was approaching, her nervous pups cautiously following behind her, blinking at Sam in curiosity and disbelief.

"Thank you. Thank you for saving my pups," she said, still trembling from the attack.

The big male rat limped out from behind a grain bag, followed by a half dozen or so who had scattered after the first shot. They gathered around Sam, snuffling and nuzzling, grooming him in gratitude.

"I am Tomas," the limping rat introduced himself. "We are so grateful to you for scaring away the sailor. Won't you please join us for dinner? Come, join my family."

Sam looked at the piles of grain scattered across the floor. It looked like sand, not at all appetizing.

"Have you seen any moths? Or maybe a mosquito?"

"Ahhhhh. You eat bugs!" Tomas replied. "Come. Where there are people, there will be food. Especially bugs. Filthy creatures. Messy. But a blessing for you, eh?"

Tomas motioned Sam towards the stairs. Sam stopped in his tracks and turned to Tomas.

"We can't go down there! What if there are more of them? With more guns?"

"No worries, my friend!" Tomas reassured him. "Most people sleep all night. It's waaaaay past suppertime for them. And the sailor you bested is probably curled up in a dark corner, licking his wounds. Come! Let's get you fed!"

Still afraid but too hungry to argue, Sam glided after Tomas, down the spiral staircase into a hot, smelly, dimly-lit hallway. Every creak and groan of the ship's hull echoed, amplified by the steel walls and floor.

"Come, this way!" Tomas scurried down the hall, his limp becoming less pronounced. Sam was glad to see the cruel kick hadn't caused any lasting damage.

Sam lifted off, staying close to the ceiling, in case he had to make another swooping attack. They rounded a corner and slipped through a pair of swinging doors. Sam heard the scratching of Tomas' claws change from tapping on the damp steel to tinkling along tile.

"Here! Sam! Bugs!" Tomas cried.

Cockroaches zipped along the floor of the ship's galley. Their little brown armored bodies moved like they were on wheels, rolling out from under cabinets and refrigerators, searching for crumbs and sticky sugar granules.

Ordinarily, Sam wouldn't have found them the

least bit appealing, but hunger makes anything with antennae and six legs a delicacy. He swooped in and scooped up the crunchy, bitter roaches. To the starving Sam, they tasted better than any moth he ever ate. He crunched each once between his teeth and swallowed them almost whole. As he filled his belly, his mind grew clearer, and the memory of his fight with the man brought a new fear.

"Tomas, do you think I killed him? I just wanted him to stop. But what if I killed him? I've never killed anything that wasn't food."

"My friend, why do you feel this guilt?" Tomas asked. "Would you rather have stood by and watched the sailor murder us all? People don't eat rats. They call us pests and hunt us for no other reason than their own selfish hoarding of food. Why, they have so much that whatever doesn't fit in their bellies, they throw into great bins and plastic bags to rot. And then they get upset when we come to dine on the food they don't even want! They poison us and shoot at us and kick us! What other animal protects its garbage? What the tiger doesn't eat, the vultures will pick clean. Whatever bits are left go to the maggots. The tiger doesn't stand around guarding a rotting carcass!"

Sam laughed at the idea of a tiger guarding a rotting capybara, an owl guarding a pellet, or a bat hovering over a leftover moth wing.

"You protected my family when we were defenseless. You could have been killed yourself, but you saw what the sailor did was wrong and cruel, and you stopped him. What you did was honorable," Tomas said. "You are a hero, Sam."

Sam thought it over. Bonnie and his mother had loved him through and through, and a large part of their lessons were about self-defense against predators. This was the first time he had to use an aggressive maneuver. He hoped he would never have to do it again.

"I understand, Tomas." Sam stood straight and tall as he spoke. "But I think that maybe we should move your family to a safer place, in case the man returns. It would be better, I think, to stay hidden for awhile. I will keep a lookout for danger."

Sam thought of Bonnie watching over him, and

of the males who guarded the pups and mothers in the nursery roost when he was still too small to fly. They'd all seemed so large and confident. Sam felt too small to fill that role for the rats. He wondered if Bonnie or the nursery guards had felt so unprepared for such a large responsibility. He began to see how so much pressure could have driven Papa Ernesto to such frightening lengths to protect his colony, even at their own peril.

Tomas did as Sam suggested and moved his family deeper within the ship's belly. It was warmer, and out of the sight of the sailors. Sam roosted above them, rustling his wings in warning

if the sailor's footsteps echoed too close to the colony. Sam loved his role of protector, but watching the family play and nap and groom

each other reminded him of the empty place in his heart that was once filled with home and family.

Tomas told Sam that his family often traveled by ship, the food was often fresh and plenty, and threats were few as long as they could manage to hide themselves well enough. The only predators were men, and they tended to be loud animals, lacking any stealth as they stomped up and down the halls and stairs. There was ample warning time during the day to run and hide, but they would sometimes become too used to the quiet at night. That's how they had been caught off-guard by the sailor with the pellet gun.

One evening, Tomas called up to Sam. "We'll be docking soon. The ship is slowing; we must be heading into port."

"We've decided to stay on board a bit longer," Tomas told Sam as the ship pulled into port. "I know you're anxious to get back to the trees, friend, but I wish you would stay. Our pups jump from the bags of rice at night, pretending to fly like you. I don't know how to tell them you're leaving."

Sam was tired of the noisy ship, and of eating the bitter cockroaches. There were few opportunities to fly, and when he did, all he saw was a black ocean reflecting the ever-changing shape of the moon. He looked forward to dry land, to hunting over open fields, and perhaps finding a roost of bats more like him, who shared his love of moths and of catching a tailwind to speed along under clouds, aiming for the horizon. Still, he would miss his friends.

"I wish you could come with me," Sam replied. "I wish you could grow wings and sail the wind instead of the sea."

The two friends considered each other. Nature had made them so different in shape, and yet so similar in heart.

"I need to find a family who can fly like me," said Sam. "I need a family who loves me, and loves each other as much as yours does."

As the day melted into night, the ship ended its journey in the port of a great city.

Sam took flight over the docks, leaving the colony of rats sleeping in a softly snoring pile. Only Tomas remained awake, winking away a tear as his winged friend headed out toward the city lights.

Chapter 5
Chelsea Morning

To Sam's delight, a great bridge stretched out before him above the water. His heart pounding in his chest, he raced toward it like a bullet. Perhaps he had found those distant cousins, perched under this magnificent bridge, lit up like all the stars in the sky.

All night, Sam followed the curves of the river

the people of London call the Thames, exploring every nook that could possibly hide a bat, and finding nothing. He saw the great clock, Big Ben, and Parliament stretched along the shore, but no sign of the colony. The glow of city lights made the stars above disappear, and the air had a faintly sooty flavor to it from the traffic below. Noise filled his ears; car horns, music, the chiming of a great bell. Sam's hopes started to dim.

Flying lower for a closer look, Sam spotted swarms of insects. They seemed hypnotized by the glowing street lamps below. He was a country bat, disoriented by the glittering lights and busy sounds of London. Distracted by the prospect of a hunt, he didn't notice the shadow below him of a stranger flying overhead.

SMACK! *"Tag! You're it!"*

Sam had just been bonked on the head by a common pipistrelle bat. She zoomed off into the night, giggling. She was no bigger than a mouse, but still rounder than Sam. She had long, curvy wings from tail to shoulders. She was round and had fluffy, deep brown fur with what looked like a pitch-black mask stretched across her snout.

"Hey! Wait! Wait for me!" Sam called. He heard her giggle in the distance and followed her between the trees, gulping up moths and other insects along the way.

"Can't catch me, Mr. Wiggle Tail!" she sang out.

"I'm not Mr. Wiggle Tail. I'm Sam!"

Her voice was musical, like Renny's. Unlike Renny, though, her voice didn't give him the shivers. There was no gritty feeling of something dark and sinister underneath. She flew like Renny, in that zigzag pattern that was one part evasive and two parts dance.

They passed a great castle, and then flittered past a statue in Belgrave Square of a strange looking man with four arms and four legs trapped inside a circle. Sam wondered if people, like bats, also came in various shapes, and hoped he never came across such a man armed with a pellet gun... or guns.

The sun was coming up. He couldn't see it cresting the horizon yet, but noted the odd statues of men cast in iron and copper beginning to glow and glint in the brightening sky. He perched on the head of Christopher Columbus and looked around for a safe place to roost for the day. Robins were chirping, and through the mist he saw a person walking along a path in the distance. He could smell the grass, and sweet peas climbing and twisting along terraces.

"Oi! Sam Wiggle Tail! Hey! Are you going to sit there watching the sun come up?" the giggly bat teased from above.

"I need to find a place to roost for the day," Sam replied. "Is there a barn or a cave close by?"

"You can come sleep over at my house! Come! Follow me, Wiggle Tail!"

Sam was annoyed by the nickname, but couldn't help but follow her. She was the first bat he'd met since the vampire colony, and he wanted to ask her about the bridge, and whether she had seen any bats like him roosting beneath it.

He followed her past Sloane Street into Cadogan Square, the cool yellow light of the sun striking happy shadows across the rows of brick houses that lined the street. This is where people lived, Sam thought, in these caves of brick with shiny windows and little boxed gardens underneath them.

They reached another brick palace, this one surrounded by wrought iron fences, with a sign on the gates that read "Draycott Hotel." They flew up and over a lovely garden filled with flowering trees and wooden benches.

The giggly bat seemed to disappear into the brick, but as Sam got closer, he saw a softball-sized hole in the wall, that lead to a crevice the size of a loaf of bread. Inside were three bats, including the giggly one, all huddled in a squishy, furry bunch.

"Come in, Sam Wiggle Tail! The sun is coming up and it's time for bed."

Sam crawled into the hole an inch at a time, half-expecting to be swallowed up inside the brick by some cruel trick of fate. But no such thing happened. Instead he was welcomed with outstretched wings by the smiling colony of three.

"Sam! These are my cousins, Neave and Gavin. And I am Jilli. And this is the finest hotel in Chelsea, the finest neighborhood in London!" Everything Jilli said was punctuated with an exclamation point. Sam couldn't help but laugh. Jilli's happy giggle was like a sneeze, infecting him with laughter he couldn't keep inside.

"Hi Jilli. And Neave. And Gavin. Thank you so much for letting me rest here with you. I've been on a ship for such a long time. I'm so happy to be on land again."

"You were on a ship?" asked Neave.

"Where did you come from?" asked Gavin.

"Why is your tail wiggly?" asked Jilli.

"Why do you talk in a funny accent?" asked Gavin.

"I'll tell you in the evening. Just... so... sleeeepy..." Sam was too exhausted to be gracious. His voice trailed off into a snore.

"I don't think I can wait that long." Neave whispered.

But Sam had already fallen into a deep sleep.

That day, Sam dreamed of the night Renny

tricked him into flying out to sea. In his dream, he didn't make it to the boat, and fell, splashing into the ocean, sinking beneath the waves. He woke shaking and coughing.

"Did you have a nightmare, Sam?" Neave asked, patting him gently. "I have them sometimes, about the Gas Man."

"Shhhhhh!" scolded Gavin. "Don't say his name! He might hear and come back!"

"Hush, Gavin," Jilli yawned. "He'll never come back. Uncle Renny made sure of that."

Sam froze. Surely she wasn't talking about Renny from the vampire bat colony? It had to be a different Renny.

"Tell us your story, Sam! You did promise us! Tell us about the ship! And your journey! And why you have a wiggly tail!" Neave cried, wiggling her bottom to mimic the movements of Sam's tail. She was practically vibrating with excitement.

Sam shook off the last bits of nightmare and began his story of the shaking of the earth, and Bonnie, and the vampire bats. Neave, Gavin, and Jilli sat, listening with rapt attention. When Sam got to the part where he met Renny, he paused, choosing his words carefully.

"I met a bat named Renny at the mine with the vampire bats. He looked like you, and had an accent like yours. I know he came there on a boat many full moons ago from the city of London, but I'm sure it couldn't be your uncle, it was so far away."

"Did he mumble? Was he... a bit, well, out of sorts?" Jilli demanded, a hint of anxiety dampening her voice.

"Well, yes. He did. Mumble, I mean." Sam kept his voice cool and careful. "And yes, he was a little out of sorts."

"Come. Let's get some breakfast," Jilli said abruptly. "Neave, Gavin, stay here and wait for us. We'll be back soon."

Before the two pups could protest, Jilli launched herself from the crack in the wall, Sam following close behind. They flew in Jilli's elegant zigzags through the city and into Hyde Park, where Jilli stopped to roost on a birch branch. Sam settled beside her.

"Renny was my uncle." Jilli had lost all the laughter from her voice. She sounded sad. "He made us laugh all the time," But Jilli's voice had no laughter in it now. "He brought us all sorts of presents he would steal from the window boxes and the park. Pinwheels that sparkled and twirled in the moonlight, roses from the Queen's garden, toffees from the candy shop, and a toy boat that a child had lost in a pond. I used to play in it and imagine I was sailing down the Thames in my own little ship. He once brought me and the other pups to a football match. The lights of the stadium brought our dinner flying right towards us. We watched David Beckham play and it was brilliant."

Sam didn't know what a queen, a football, or a David Beckham was, but Jilli made it all sound like magic.

"Sometimes in the summer when it was very hot, Renny would bring us to the theatre through a broken vent, and we would see people in moving pictures, bigger than a house! They were called movies, and the theatres were always cool and dark. Our favorite was about a bat who could turn into a man with a long, red cape and scare people off with his fangs. Renny would pretend to be the bat-man and chase us around our flat.

"Back then, we lived in the eaves of a little house on Fernshaw Road. My roost had lived there for generations with a nice little family of people who never seemed bothered by our being there. We kept the yard free of midges, and they never shooed us away. The house was passed from grandmother to grandson, until the last member of the family grew old and passed away. The house stood empty for only one turn of the moon before a new family moved in, and they didn't like us one bit." Jilli paused, as if it had suddenly become hard to speak. "And then the Gas Man came."

She swallowed hard and her eyes welled up with tears. Sam reached out for Jilli with an outstretched wing to gather her close to him, like his mother had done when he was just a pup. He knew what grief was, what a deep loss felt like. He had seen that loss in Bonnie's eyes, and felt it in his own heart, and now he recognized it in Jilli.

"It was late in the morning, and we were all

asleep when the Gas Man appeared in the window. He wore a mask, so we couldn't see his cowardly face. He had a tank on his back, and a long, shiny tube in his hand. That's where the poison gas came from, in big clouds that filled our house and made our eyes and lungs burn. We coughed and cried, and tried to fly, but our chests felt like a fire had been lit inside. We were dying."

Jilli took a long, deep breath, followed by a tiny cough, and looked deep into Sam's eyes.

"It's still there. Whenever I take a deep breath, I can feel the itchy poison down in the bottom of my lungs, like a scar," she said. "But then Renny swooped in and fought with the Gas Man. He scratched at his mask and his hair, and sent the Gas Man falling back down his ladder, onto his lazy, cowardly bum! Uncle Renny hollered to us to hold our breath, and I tried, but I couldn't stop coughing. My eyes burned, and I couldn't see. All I could hear was the crying of my family, the weak beating of wings, and the Gas Man crying out in pain outside the window. I couldn't quite sort it all out. There was so much noise, and my throat and eyes were burning so. I was all turned around and couldn't find my way out of it. Then there was a hot, burning pain in my wing. Uncle Renny bit into me and tossed me toward the window, into the fresh air. I gulped it down like fresh water. And then, when my head cleared, I realized I was lying on a pile of bodies."

Sam bit his lip so as not to cry out. He had been missing his family for so long, but he hadn't actually seen them die in front of his eyes the way Jilli had. He didn't want to think about them suffering, but Jilli's story brought him back to the desert, wondering what it had been like for everyone in his family when the earth shook, and how frightened they all must have been. He didn't know how he would go on if he had heard them cry in pain, he didn't know if he could have been as strong as Jilli, or Renny, for that matter.

"Gavin and Neave were just tiny babies, twins. They could barely fly at all. Uncle Renny found them—he grabbed Neave by the nape and flew her down to the hedgerow, and dropped her in. He went back for Gavin, and then for me. I was too big to carry, and Uncle Renny pushed me to the edge and yelled at me to fly for my life. Then he pushed me. I thought I was going to crash right into the ground, but caught one of those blessed gusts of wind and rode it to the hedgerow. Gavin and Neave were there, struggling to breathe, and crying for their mama. Renny stayed behind, trying to find survivors, holding his breath, but there was no one left alive."

Renny had been a hero, once. He had risked his life to save his family. He had once been noble, he had once been loved, and had loved others in return. Sam couldn't quite wrap his mind around it.

"I watched Uncle Renny leap from the window and fall to the ground, coughing all the way down. The Gas Man was lying on the grass next to his ladder, and moaning, and Uncle Renny was half-hopping, half-crawling toward him. When my uncle got there, he lunged and bit him right on his ear. The Gas Man flailed and cried out, slapping at Renny, but he wouldn't let go. I could hear him snarling through his teeth, calling the Gas Man a murderer and coward.

"The Gas Man finally tore Renny away, along with a piece of his own ear. My uncle tumbled across the garden and slammed into the stone bird-bath. He didn't move, and I thought he was dead. There was nothing I could do, not really. I just snuggled Neave and Gavin close, and tried to comfort them as best I could."

Sam listened intently. Maybe it had been the gas, or the bump on the head, or maybe the grief of not being able to save the whole colony. Or, he thought, maybe all of it had combined to drive Renny mad.

Jilli continued her story. Renny had stayed with Jilli and the twins, guarding them from cats and birds, attacking anything that got too close to the hedgerow. Jilli hunted at night for all of them, while Renny paced and mumbled to himself. Eventually, while out hunting, Jilli found the crevice in the Draycott, and the twins were strong enough to fly on their own to the new home.

But Renny's insanity was getting worse, and his

anger at humans was putting them all at risk. He would swoop low and frighten the hotel guests out walking in the garden in the evening. Jilli feared they would be discovered, and the Gas Man would return to finish them all. It broke her heart to do so, but Gavin and Neave depended on her to teach them how to hunt and avoid predators, and she had to make a choice between the lives of her young cousins and her mad uncle.

"I ran him off. I cried all the way to the river, biting at him, chasing him off. He saved us. And I had to run him off. It was the hardest thing I ever had to do, Sam." Her words trailed off, and she dropped her head and wept.

Sam felt his hate and confusion melt into pity and forgiveness. However crazy and murderous Renny was now, he was once a beloved uncle, a protector, a hero.

"Is he better now?" Jilli asked. "Does he remember us?" And then she whispered, "Do you think he's forgiven me?"

Sam was startled at the thought of someone else wanting Renny's forgiveness, just as Sam was beginning to feel it himself. He stood as straight as he could, and looked Jilli in the eye.

"I don't think he remembers much of anything, Jilli. He still mumbles a lot, and seems a bit confused. But he's warm and safe with his new colony, and he brought me dinner when I was hungry. He took care of me."

Sam felt a little uncomfortable. He told himself he hadn't exactly lied, but he knew he hadn't told her the whole truth, either. Still, he thought, it was a kindness to let her know that her uncle was safe and sound. The Renny who'd attacked the Gas Man and taken such good care of Jilli and the pups was lost forever. There was no need to tarnish his memory.

"I'm so grateful to your uncle for saving you, Jilli. And I think he'd be proud of you for taking care of Gavin and Neave. You are a hero, too. You did the right thing. You protected those who couldn't protect themselves."

The two bats sat in the tree for the rest of the night, watching clouds pass over the moon, telling each other what each cloud's shape looked like.

Sam thought they were shaped like tasty moths, and Jilli thought they looked like great bats watching over them from above. Gradually, they drifted closer together and cuddled sweetly. Sam thought that perhaps, if he could not find his colony, he would like to stay with Jilli and the twins, that Chelsea could become his home. He liked the smell of the rain, and the lovely gardens. He could even become accustomed to the sounds of the traffic and people. Plus, midges were actually quite filling, if a bit flavorless.

"Jilli?" Sam whispered, careful to not wake the sleeping twins.

"Hmmmm?"

"Would it be okay, do you think, if I stayed with you forever? Like a family?"

It had been two full moons since Sam arrived on Jilli's side of the Atlantic, and he felt at peace. His dreams of the bridge over the river and his lost colony were fewer, and less vivid.

Jilli half-opened her drowsy eyes. "You *are* family, Wiggle Tail."

And so it went, night after night. The four bats

would fly out to hunt, sometimes together, sometimes alone. They would share stories every dawn, snuggled in a happy, soft pile of fur, wings, and claws before falling asleep for the day.

That is, until the terrible cat incident occurred.

If Sam had known what a calendar was, or how to read one, he would have known it was his birthday. It had been a year since Sam was born in a cave in Southern California. But since Sam had no knowledge of calendars, he busied himself with his hunt. His only worries were making sure he had a full belly and getting back to the crevice in the brick wall before dawn.

He sat perched on the edge of a birdbath in the park, taking a sip of rainwater and watching the reflection of the moon ripple on the surface. He should have been paying better attention to his surroundings, as he'd been taught to do by his mother and Bonnie. Had he been paying attention, he might have seen the black and silver tabby cat sneaking up on him, her eyes glowing amber in the dark.

The tabby pounced, and Sam cried out in surprise as he was pinned to the ground. All he saw were fangs and all he heard was the hiss of the cat bearing down on him. He cried out again as the tabby clawed at his belly. As the cat's face came close to Sam's, he gathered all of his strength, curled one clawed wing, and struck out at the cat's nose with his thumb, drawing blood. The tabby cried out in surprise and pain, and released Sam just long enough for him to lift off. She took a final swipe at him, but a lucky gust of wind pulled him out of reach.

Sam lit on a tree branch and inspected his wounds with horror. He was bleeding and he didn't know what to do to make it stop, or whether it ever would. The slices on his belly stung, and he felt his body getting colder, and it hurt to shiver. He gripped onto the branch and collected himself. All he wanted to do was get back to the wall, so that he could fall safely asleep in the soft pile of his new family, and tell the great story about surviving the terrible cat attack. Sam, cold and sleepy, closed his eyes and imagined being warm and safe in the crevice.

The next time Sam opened his eyes, he was staring at the big, black, wet nose of a beagle, which was sniffing at him and pushing at him with his great snout.

Sometime during the night, Sam had fallen from the branch, but he'd been too weak and injured to realize it. Even now, he could barely muster fright. A second beagle trotted up next to the first, and sniffed at Sam as well.

"Rudy! Harrison! What have you got there?"

Sam had trouble focusing, but recognized the shape of a man standing over him. Sam was rarely awake this late in the morning. He would have felt confused and sluggish in the best of times, but his injuries made it worse.

The man reached down and grabbed the dogs by their collars, pulling them away from Sam's crumpled shape.

"Poor little man." The man pulled off his houndstooth cap, and scooped Sam up. The cap was warm and dry, and strangely comforting. The man gingerly wrapped his hat around Sam, enveloping him in warmth, and the scent of bergamot and spice. Sam closed his eyes again and took a long nap.

The man who found Sam was no enemy of bats.

When he arrived home, he lined a shoebox with an old t-shirt and placed Sam inside. He put medicine on Sam's wounds, and wrapped a bandage around him. He poked a few holes in the box's lid and gently touched Sam's head before placing the lid on the box, giving Sam a dark, safe, warm bed. Sam was too ill to protest being handled, and too sleepy to be frightened for more than a moment before his eyes snapped shut and his senses faded into dream.

The man fed the dogs their breakfast, filled a

thermos with tea and packed some biscuits. Then, tucking the shoebox under his arm, he set out for a long drive to the docks. Along the way, he told Sam stories of his grandson and daughter, who lived on the Isle of Wight, and how nice it was to have an excuse to visit. Sam could hear the man speaking, his voice muffled by the box. Sam didn't speak Man, and the man didn't speak Bat, but the man's voice was deep and kind and soothing, so Sam responded now and then with a squeak just to let the man know he was listening. By the time they got to the dock, the man had told Sam his entire life story, and Sam hadn't understood one word of it.

A ferry took them across the channel to the island. The sensation of being on a boat, rocking along the waves, reminded Sam of Tomas and the rat family. He was jostled when the man picked up the box and carried him onto dry land. He heard the echo of footsteps on wood, and the crunch of the gravel under the man's feet. The excited voices of people called out, and gulls cried overhead.

The lid of the box opened a crack, and a pair of

wide eyes appeared over the edge of his shoebox. A boy gasped and smiled warmly at Sam. He would have smiled back at the boy, but he was so weak and so sleepy he could only manage a tiny squeak and a yawn. Sam slept fitfully for the rest of the journey to the Isle of Wight Bat Hospital.

When Sam woke again, his bandages and bedding had been changed. He was in a wooden box, toasty warm. He could smell food and water close by, and saw a moonbeam spilling like a spotlight through a vent, onto one of the walls. There was a slight bitter, metallic taste in his mouth. He heard the scratching, squeaking, and fluttering of other bats, very close, all around him.

"Hello?" Sam called. "Can anyone hear me?"

"Hallooooo..." came an answer, and then several more.

"Hallo there, young fellow!" from an old male voice.

"Cheers!" came a high pitched squeak.

"Wot's your name, love?" said a younger girl.

"I'm Sam. Please, can someone tell me where I am?"

"You're in hospital, love," replied the younger girl. "Are you ill?"

"There was a cat." Sam shivered, remembering the attack. "She scratched my belly, and I was bleeding. And then there was a man, and he kept me safe."

"Poor little man," the old male sympathized. "The doctors will make you right as rain, you'll see. Just take your medicine and eat your mealworms and you'll be flying again in no time 'tall."

"Just as soon as you're better, the doctors will set you out on your own," the younger female added.

Sam thought about it. It was people taking care of him, and these other injured bats? People were feeding him and keeping him warm?

"Do you live here on the island, Sam?" the old male asked.

"I don't really live anywhere at the moment. I was staying with friends in Chelsea, I came from the desert, and then I stayed in the jungle, and then there was a boat, and that's how I ended up here. But I'm hoping to stay with my friends in Chelsea, forever."

"Poor dear must have a terrible fever," the younger female whispered, as if Sam couldn't hear her.

"What's a desert?" the old male whispered back.

It did sound like a fantastic story, he supposed, and decided that it was best to keep the details to himself.

Over the next few days, he was visited often by the man and the woman. They changed the dressings on his wounds, gave him medicine through a small hollow straw made of glass, and gave him fresh food and water. Each night Sam ate a bit more than he'd eaten the night before, and felt stronger with each passing night. His naps became shorter, and he started to feel restless. His wounds stopped itching so much.

He was tired of eating mealworms. At night he roosted, clutching the wire across the roof of his cage. He spoke with the other bats as they came and went. There was a pair of babies who had fallen from their roosts and were suckling milk from sponges, various victims of cat attacks, and one little fellow who'd had a run-in with a toy airplane.

Finally, the night came when the man and woman brought Sam inside their cottage and set him free to fly. Sam soared and flitted around the room, looking for a way out. He tried every window and every door. It was terribly frustrating, and he found a corner to roost while he thought it over.

The man chuckled and spoke to the woman, who seemed to agree with him. He walked over to Sam, and picked him up off the picture frame he was clinging to. Sam wriggled and squeaked.

The man went outside and tossed Sam up into the air, as if he was setting a balloon free. Sam took off like a bullet, unsure where he was going, but enjoying every moth and midge along the way. Above, the sky stretched out before him, limitless. He looped back once to say goodbye to the kind man and woman who had cared for him, and to tell the other bats that he was free.

"GOODBYE SAM!!" the bats called from their sickbeds.

Sam soared as high as he could, trying to find the city lights of Chelsea, any familiar landmark at all. He tried to navigate by the stars, but rainclouds lay like a wet wool blanket, covering the constellations.

Sam spied a barn off in the distance. He darted towards it, hoping to find a local bat who could direct him back to the Draycott. He couldn't wait to reunite with Jilli and the twins and tell them that people had helped him, that they weren't all horrid murderers like the Gas Man, that there were people who loved bats and cared for them when they were ill.

The barn, however, was absent of bats, as were the surrounding grounds. It was beginning to rain softly, and Sam headed in through a window to watch the clouds pass over the moon, guessing the shapes, as he and Jilli had done so many nights before.

A deep, throaty voice called from below. "Hallo there, little bat." A bay shire horse tossed his mane out of his eyes and gave Sam a wink.

"Hello!" Sam called down to the horse. "I'm trying to find my way back to a place called Chelsea, and I'm lost. Do you know which way it is?"

"Chelsea?" A new voice spoke in the darkness, and another horse came into view, jet black with shaggy white fur on her legs that looked like fringed boots. "That's on the mainland, little bat. You'll need to take the ferry across. Oh, hello—I'm Grace. This is my brother, Noah. We're taking the ferry to the mainland in the morning, and you're welcome to come with us if you like."

Grace tossed her mane and cleared her throat. "Stupid bitey flies," she muttered, obviously irritated. Clouds of midges hovered around the horses, taking bites and swarming, and then biting again.

"We came for a show, and we're stuck in this awful barn for the night. Someone forgot to pack the fly spray, looks like," Noah explained, furiously switching his tail.

"My name is Sam, and I'm lucky to have met you. I'm terribly hungry, and I would be happy to eat those flies that are bothering you so!"

"Lovely!" Grace cried. "Now, what you should do is climb up under my mane before dawn, and hide. They'll lead Noah and me into a cart, and you'll be safe with us until we land on the other side."

"Right. And please feel free to eat as many of those stupid git flies as you like," Noah grumbled, still itchy from the swarm.

Sam chased flies all night, allowing the horses to sleep comfortably, and when dawn approached, he followed Grace's suggestion and hid under her mane to hitch a ride back to the mainland. Snuggled up against the powerful neck with his eyes closed and the coarse mane tickling his cheek, Sam was sure he'd be back at the Draycott playing with Jilli in the gardens by dusk.

When they arrived on the mainland, Sam was still fast asleep in Grace's mane. By the time they reached London, it was the middle of the day, and no time for bats to be awake. The horses, however, had other ideas and were ready to leave the confines of their trailer for some fresh morning air and breakfast. Their stamping and fidgeting shook Sam loose. If he hadn't let out a surprised squeak, Grace might have accidentally trampled him under her hooves.

"Well, good morning to you, little Sam!" Noah said. "We've arrived!"

Sam squinted up at the vents where a cool clouded sunbeam poured into the trailer. "It's the middle of the day..." he yawned, and flitted up onto Grace's head to peek out of the window. The street outside was very busy, with people milling about on the sidewalk, chatting and laughing and yelling over the noise of cars and honking horns.

Sam sniffed the air and found it unfamiliar. This was not Chelsea.

"We're going to be leaving soon, going out to the countryside, away from the city, back to our fields, Sam," Grace warned. "We're stuck in traffic, and you should probably get out here, before we get too far away from your Chelsea."

"I'm not sure how to get there from here," Sam worried. "And I can't fly very well in the day-time."

"You can take the underground!" Noah ex-claimed. "They're tunnels under the streets. People take them to get where they want to go! And they're very dark, black as pitch. I took a train once when I was just a young horse. You go into the tunnel, and the cars move very fast, and then when you come out, you'll be exactly in the pace you want to be! It's simply magical. Just get inside, wish for Chelsea, and there you'll be in no time at all."

Sam had his doubts. After all, he had wished very hard for his mama to return for him, and when that hadn't come true, he'd wished to find the bridge over the river. Wishing didn't seem to do much good. But he still had hope, and Noah's reassurance that it would work out just fine.

"Well, even if it doesn't take you to Chelsea,

you'll be no worse off than you are now," Grace pointed out. "Lost is lost, but this way, you have a shot at getting back home."

Home. The word filled Sam with warmth. He could be back at the Draycott in just a few minutes, snuggled safely in the crevice with Jilli and the twins.

"Goodbye, and thanks again!" Sam waved with a wing, jumped, and darted out through the vent.

As Sam swooped over the crowd of travelers outside the station, he heard a few screams. Bright lightning flashes disoriented him as people tried to take his picture with their cellphone cameras. A woman ducked for cover as he swooped into the station just inches above her head. Sam paid her no mind as he clicked and squeaked through the station, trying to gauge where the opening to the tunnel was.

SWISH! Sam was almost swept from the air by a cleaning woman and her broom. Remembering the tale of Cousin Edith's encounter with the

Broom Wife, Sam flew higher near the ceiling, scoping out the station. People were pointing at him, some laughing and clapping, and some shuddering in fear.

Sam clicked at the air once more, but could only hear the return echo of the walls, glass, and shops surrounding him. He swooped down and hid behind a black schedule board, collecting his thoughts. Beneath him, travelers hustled by with large rolling luggage. There were porters pushing large carts filled with all sorts of baggage. Sam took a deep breath, waited for the right moment, closed his eyes, and let go of the black schedule board. He plopped down in a pile of black suitcases, camouflaged and unnoticed by passers-by.

Sam cautiously opened one eye, as if being able to see would make him visible. He burrowed deep into the luggage, taking refuge in an unzipped pocket on a large green suitcase while he tried to hatch an escape plan. However quickly he wanted to find Jilli, he knew he was safer in the sky. At least from there, he could look down for the statues and row houses that lined his neighborhood.

Before he could collect his thoughts, the porter's cart stopped, and he felt himself being lifted up and set down on a hard surface. He dared not peek out of the pocket, for fear of being seen by an unfriendly person. He heard the muffled sounds of men and women speaking, more luggage being unloaded from carts, and footsteps clicking and stomping on a tile floor. He tried to look on the better side of things—at least it was dark.

Just then, there was a loud CLANG! Sam waited until he no longer heard footsteps near him or felt the jostling of luggage being tossed about. He popped his head out of the pocket, and found himself in a dark metal cave, near the bottom of a pile of suitcases and boxes; he could hardly believe he hadn't been squashed. Sam hopped up on top of a rack, and peered outside for a better look. A jolt sent him tumbling back down the mountain of luggage, as his metal cave started to move.

When he steadied himself, he could see that he was moving without flapping his wings. It reminded him of being in the car of the man who had taken him to the hospital.

He watched as the train moved through the station, watched the shadows of the rafters sliding by faster and faster, and then suddenly they shot out into a blinding, wonderful light. They were outside! Exhausted, Sam perched upside-down under the rack, and closed his eyes for a moment, hoping that the next time the doors opened, he'd be in Chelsea. As he drifted off, he whispered to himself, "I wish I was home... I wish I was home..."

Sam had no way of knowing that he and the luggage were no longer in the Underground. This was no ordinary tunnel—it was the Chunnel, the thirty-two mile undersea rail that connects England and France. Sam's train was on a nonstop trip into Paris.

Chapter 6
The Stone Bats of Notre Dame

When Sam next opened his eyes, the train had stopped, and the doors were opening. He tucked himself back into the safety of the pocket, hoping he'd be rolled out the same way he was rolled in. Sure enough, he was tossed onto a luggage cart and driven through the station. When he felt brave enough, he peeked out and saw the same scenery, passengers running and milling about in the grand station. It all looked the same to Sam; people, people, and more people. Some would be kind, others cruel. Sam decided he wasn't taking any risks until he saw an opening to the outdoors.

As the cart rattled through the station, beeping and swerving around all types of obstacles, Sam was surprised by a sudden rush of fresh air. The smell was so intoxicating, he felt helpless to stop himself from flying toward it. Just as in London, the people going about their business in the Gare du Nord in Paris were shocked to see a bat darting about inside the station. Some screamed, others laughed as Sam soared up toward the windows and then swirled down toward the opening where he caught the scent of tree pollen being carried on the breeze.

Out he went, veering east and away from the setting sun. He let the wind carry him upwards to look at the city below. Confusion furrowed Sam's brow. It was all different.

From up high, Paris stretched out before him. It was lovely, busy, and bright. Instead of the bridge that had first greeted him in London, a great narrow iron tower, all lit up, stretched skyward. Traffic moved through city streets in a strange rhythm, like blood flowing through veins, though Sam could see no identifiable heart pumping them along. Beneath him, bridge after bridge after bridge stretched over a river choked with boat traffic, and Sam felt his heart flutter.

He wondered how far from Chelsea he had traveled, and in which direction. The position of the constellations overhead told him he hadn't traveled very far. At least, not as far as he had when he left Argentina.

Sam flew toward the great tower, intending to perch and decide whether he needed to find a way back on the train, back to London, Chelsea, and Jilli. As he got closer, he saw a familiar movement.

Bats. Fluttering in the sky around the tower, he saw bats.

"Of course!" Sam shouted. "Moths!"

Sam's belly rumbled. The bright lights on the tower would attract moths, and where there were moths, bats wouldn't be far behind.

Adrenaline shot through Sam's body and made his fur stand straight on end. Could they be part of the colony from his mother's tale? If so, maybe he could find his way back to Chelsea to collect Jilli and the twins; they'd be safe with his family. Sam's mind raced as he navigated toward the tower.

As Sam drew closer, he could see that these bats weren't like him, nor were they like any of the other bats he'd met on his journey. These bats circled the tower like birds, soaring in smooth dips and uplifts. Jilli and the twins zigzagged through the sky as though they were moths. And these bats had fuzzy, white bellies, and no wiggly tails. Still, they were bats, and they were eating moths, not blood.

Sam approached cautiously, scooping up some moths on the way. He lit on a metal bar to watch the bats swirling around the tower, and find a way to introduce himself.

The bats dipped lower and lower, swooping over the crowds of people at the base of the tower. Sam watched as some screamed and ran away, while others laughed and snapped photographs. It was just like the scenes he'd caused himself in the train stations, only these bats seemed to be teasing the people on purpose.

"Showoffs," said a velvety voice from above.

Sam looked up, surprised. Three little bats were perched on a beam just above him. He had been so focused on the bats in flight the trio had gone unnoticed.

Sam hopped up on the beam beside them. "Hi!"

The three white-bellied bats stared at him with wide, black eyes.

"What sort of bat are you?" asked the one in the middle. "You look like a mouse with wings." The bats on each end nodded in agreement.

Sam blinked. He didn't think he looked like a mouse at all, and he couldn't tell whether the trio was trying to insult him, or was just curious about his tail.

"I'm just Sam," he said. "I come from the desert."

"Well, Just Sam, welcome to Paris," said the middle bat. "I am

Jacqueline, but everyone calls me Coco. These are Aurore and Sylvie, my friends."

Coco didn't tell Sam which was which, and neither did Aurore or Sylvie. They only grinned and said, "Bonjour" in perfect unison, leaving Sam still without a clue.

"What brings you in from the desert?" asked Coco.

Sam could hardly think how to start. With the earthquake, or his long flight with Bonnie, or the jungle and Renny and the container ship? Or maybe just with the train that had brought him here to the tower?

"I don't know quite where to begin..." Sam admitted.

All three leaned in toward Sam, their faces alight with curiosity. "The most interesting stories always begin with those very words," said the bat to Coco's right, who was either Aurore or Sylvie.

Sam began at the very beginning, with the last moth he ate before the earthquake took his family. By the time he got to the tale of the terrible cat that almost killed him, the four bats who had been teasing the people below had settled in on the perch beside the trio, and were listening with rapt attention.

"No one survives a cat attack," said one of the bats Sam hadn't yet met.

"I did." Sam straightened up and displayed the jagged scar on his belly as proof. "I went to hospital, and people saved me."

Their jaws dropped in wonder. It reminded Sam of the way the twins looked at him when he spoke of Bonnie, and learning to fly like an owl.

"Sam, you said your family lives under a bridge, over a river," said Coco. "Have you looked under the bridges over the Seine?"

Coco pointed toward the east. Sam looked down at the river, curling wide and beautiful from east to west, with the golden lights of the city dancing across its surface.

"The sun will be up, soon," remarked Sylvie/Aurore.

"Why don't you come stay with us, Sam?" invited the bat who had questioned Sam about the cat attack. "We can help you search under the bridges in the evening, tomorrow."

Sam smiled widely at his newfound friends, and lifted off with them toward their daytime refuge. They darted across the city toward a domed building surrounded by trees.

"It's an observatory," Coco explained as she soared just above Sam. "Where people go to look at the sky."

"Why can't they just look up?" asked Sam.

Coco shrugged. "I don't think they can see very well. So they make tall buildings to get them closer to the stars."

All seven bats plus Sam darted into a wooden box affixed to an old tree in the center of a neat lawn bordered by walking paths leading to the observatory. The bats groomed each other and told Sam their stories as they settled in to sleep for the day.

It turned out that Sam was not the only bat who had come from a faraway place. There was Giorgio, who had been born in a land called Italy, and got lost in a storm one evening. Peter had come from Germany with his family after their tree was cut down to make room for someone's new garage.

Pierre and Sebastien were brothers who had grown up in France. They seemed smitten with Sylvie and Aurore, nuzzling the girls' chins while flashing silly, lovesick grins. Sylvie and Aurore pretended to be oblivious, but would occasionally exhale a contended sigh of encouragement.

Coco was asleep before Sam could ask her where she was born, and Sam followed her shortly after with a gentle snore.

The next evening, the group set out to search under all the bridges of Paris for signs of Sam's family.

They headed back toward the tower, following the river and looking for signs of roosts, but finding none. Sometimes they skimmed over the water, making ripples as their wings brushed the surface, and scooping up insects along the way. Sometimes they soared higher, passing over grand buildings, and from up on high Sam saw one with a shining gold dome that reminded him of the observatory. The whole of Paris seemed to twinkle with golden light, as if the sky had turned upside-down and all the stars had shaken loose, sprinkling the city with their sparkling glow.

Pierre chased Aurore, or possibly Sylvie, along the river, scooping up water with his wings and splashing her. The bats swirled and swooped under every bridge they came to, but the only bats they met along the way were ones without tails, and none knew of a colony of bats that looked like Sam.

Sam caught up to Giorgio, Coco, and Peter, who were perched just under a stone bridge, where the river began to split. They were resting from the hunt, their bellies full. The others had been so busy playing that they had forgotten to eat, and had flown off to hunt a little longer.

"I don't think we'll find your family here," the usually quiet Peter said.

"Look!" mumbled Giorgio. A piece of straw danged from between his fangs. "I have a tail! I could be your brother!"

Coco sighed. "A tail grows from your bottom, not your mouth."

"I though his face WAS his bottom!" quipped Giorgio, and laughed so hard at his own joke that he was in danger of choking on the straw. Everyone but Peter, who was thinking, snickered at Giorgio's comeuppance.

"You know, there is a bat nearby who may know how to find them," Peter offered. "He's the oldest, ugliest bat in all the world, and he knows everything that has ever happened under the moon."

"Here we go," groaned Coco.

"As I was saying," Peter began again, glaring at Coco, "the oldest bat in all the world lives in Notre Dame—it's that cathedral, just after the split in the river. The Oldest, Ugliest Bat in All the World is completely deaf, so he can't hunt any longer. He steals whatever he finds in spider's webs, including the spiders. Because he's so old, and because he eats such terrible food, he has become so terrifyingly ugly that a single look at him could turn you into stone. And that is where the Cathedral's bat statues come from, you see."

Peter dropped his voice to a whisper. "They were once perfectly normal bats until they caught a glimpse of the Oldest, Ugliest Bat in All the World. Now they're perched there as gargoyles forever, frozen in terror."

"Every time you tell this story, it gets a little bit more ridiculous." Coco rolled her eyes. "Look Sam, there is a very old bat in the cathedral, and like you, he's seen much of the world." She glared at Peter, "And he's not completely deaf. I think it's a good idea to ask him about your missing family. He can at least give you some good advice. The old can be very wise."

Sam though about Papa Ernesto, who seemed more frightened than wise. Peter's spooky story reminded him of the terrifying tales the vampire bat would tell to keep his colony inside the mine. But just as Bonnie was different from other owls, perhaps this old bat would be different from Papa Ernesto.

"I'd like to talk to him," Sam told Coco. "I miss my desert, and how sweet the moths were. I miss how much brighter the stars were there."

"YOU'LL HAVE TO YELL LIKE THIS," hollered Giorgio, almost scaring Sam into letting go of his perch and dropping headfirst into the river. "HE REALLY IS QUITE DEAF."

Peter and Coco, annoyed, both shook their heads. Watching them, Sam thought what a lovely couple they would make if only they'd stop sniping at each other. He looked down at the water rushing by underneath them, and wondered if there was another bat, just like him, watching a river just like this one, with the reflection of the moon rippling on the surface.

The bats crossed the river to the cathedral. When they reached it, Sam was awestruck at the huge, stone gothic building sprawling along the river's edge, adorned with giant, leering faces of monsters carved from stone. Sam knew that these were really sculptures from some human's worst nightmare, and not actual bats suffering a magical affliction caused by fright. Still, the building was spooky and the story had gotten under his skin.

"Well?" Peter asked. "Go and see for yourself! If you turn to stone, don't say I didn't warn you!"

Coco shook her head and whispered to Sam, " If you're frightened, I will go with you, if you'd like."

Sam set his jaw. He didn't want anyone to think he was afraid. "Thanks, Coco, but I'll be fine."

He launched himself toward the building, landing right on the head of one of the gargoyles. Then he turned and stuck his tongue out at Peter, who pretended he didn't see Sam mocking him.

"WE'LL WAIT FOR YOU RIGHT HERE!" screamed Giorgio. "REMEMBER TO YELL LOUD LIKE THIS OR HE WON'T HEAR YOU!"

Sam puffed out his chest, trying to make himself look bigger and stronger than he actually was, and began exploring every crevice along the cathedral's exterior. His claws hugged the walls, and he clenched his eyes shut at every echo that bounced off the cold stone.

And then, out of nowhere, he found himself face-to-face with The Oldest, Ugliest Bat in All the World.

Sam screamed... and froze. His nose twitched and he frantically started testing his facial movements. What if Peter was right?

He made funny faces stretching his snout and raising his eyebrows. He stuck out his tongue, did a back flip, and danced a jig. Every muscle still worked.

The Oldest, Ugliest Bat raised a shaky, wizened claw at Sam and wheezed in a dry, elderly voice, "RAAAABIEEEEEESSSSSSS!!!!" That was immediately followed by a hacking cough.

"What?" Sam asked. He didn't understand what the old bat meant.

"RABIES!" cried the old bat. He ducked behind a gargoyle, trying to hide.

"I DON'T KNOW WHAT RABIES IS!" bellowed Sam.

The old bat peeked out from under one wrinkled wing. He took a closer look at Sam, who was no longer dancing about like a lunatic. "Perhaps you don't have rabies," he said. "It's the bat plague, son. Makes you act crazy and then you fly up into the sun and roast. Terribly contagious."

"I NEED YOUR HELP!" hollered Sam. "I'M LOST."

The old bat studied Sam for a moment, and then stretched out a wing.

"Come with me, then, son. Come inside out of the cold and let's see what we can do about your situation."

Victor led Sam through a crevice into a small nook. "My name is Victor," he told Sam. "Welcome to my home."

A tiny sliver of moonlight shone through, just enough to show Sam that Victor had made quite a nest for himself. Bits of plastic, yarn, objects that sparkled, and a shard from a looking-glass.

Victor made himself comfortable in a pile of straw and told Sam his story.

"I made the mistake of roosting in a bell when I was a young bat, just about your age, and was struck deaf one Easter Sunday. I've lived here ever since. It's safer here. I can't hear owls sneaking up on me anymore."

He pointed at the jagged scar on Sam's belly from the cat attack, and then towards his own face. Sam leaned toward the old bat and saw a deep scar twisting down his face.

"I'm so sorry," Sam whispered.

Victor couldn't hear Sam's words, but he could see the sympathy and respect in his eyes. He reached out and patted Sam on the head.

"No worries, little one. I'm quite happy here.

Plenty of moths stumble this way. I have enough to eat, and I spend my nights watching the moon and stars," explained Victor. "Now. You say you're lost? Where is it that you need to go?"

Sam opened his mouth, then snapped it shut with a click. He didn't know where he needed to go.

He could ask how to get back to Chelsea, where he'd been so happy with Jilli and the twins. But Chelsea was cold and rainy, and he could never quite get the feeling of dampness out of his nose.

He could ask if Victor knew of the bridge where his family lived, but Sam thought that perhaps the story was just that; a story. For all he knew, the same earthquake that took his cave could have shaken the bridge right into the river, washing it away.

Sam looked out at the stars, dim and fuzzy-looking in the city sky, and longed to see them again over the desert sky, shining crisp and bright. His desert sky. He thought about the sweetness of the moths, and the warm winds lifting him up toward a full desert moon.

"I want to go home?" Sam asked himself, not realizing he said the words aloud.

"I can't hear you, son."

Sam straightened his jaw. "I WANT TO GO HOME!"

Victor chuckled and leaned back in his nest. "Well, it would help if I knew where your home was. Then maybe I could help you find your way back."

But Sam didn't know where his home was, anymore. The world was a much bigger place than

he could have imagined when he started his journey with Bonnie. He took a deep breath, and exhaled slowly.

"I've traveled so far, Victor. There was a boat, and a train, and the world seems to just go on forever. I don't know how far I've come."

"The world doesn't go on forever, son." Victor sounded very sure of himself. "It goes around in a circle. If you just keep going, you'll eventually get back to where you started."

Sam raised his brow, puzzled. "I don't understand."

"Look." Victor pointed at the sky. "The moon, it is round. So is the sun. And so is this land where we perch and hunt. I've watched the sky for a long time. We're turning in it, every day. We turn toward the sun and it is dawn... but on the other side of this ball we're living on, it must be night."

Victor turned and rummaged through the pile of scraps behind him.

"Ah! Here it is!"

He turned and pushed something toward Sam. A small red marble came rolling toward him along the stone floor. Victor reached out, stopping it with the tip of one wing. He rolled it around in a circle, back to the pile of scraps.

"The stars seem to move past us, like clouds being blown in the wind. But I've watched them for a long time, Sam, while I wait for moths to fly close enough to catch from my roost!" Victor smiled, his eyes crinkled, and he wiggled his crooked nose. "The shapes the stars make in the sky make patterns, and I've watched them come and go, over and over again. Sometimes there are stars that don't twinkle, a blue one, a red one, a bright one... and we turn with them, you see? So if the moon is round, and the sun is round, then we, too, are living on something round."

Victor rolled the marble around, again. "Like this. You understand me?"

Sam had always thought that that the sun and moon chased each other through the sky, trying to catch each other, the way Pierre chased Aurore/Sylvie. He liked the idea of the world spinning through the sky like a marble. If that were true, and Victor was right, Sam thought, he might have traveled far enough around it to be closer to where he started from...

"When you started your journey, in which direction did you fly?" Victor asked.

On and on throughout the night, Victor asked questions. He asked Sam how long he'd flown, and what he could remember about the sky above. Sam answered as best he could, and while the old bat scratched his chin, Sam would venture outside the cathedral to catch moths for the both of them to munch. Sam's voice became scratchy and hoarse from all the yelling.

It was almost sunrise when Victor raised his wings, cocked his head to the left and exclaimed, "*Bof*! The world, it seems, is much fatter than I thought it was!"

"What does that mean?" croaked Sam.

"It means," replied Victor, "that by the time you travel back to where you came from, you will be as old as I am."

Sam crumpled down onto the cold stone floor and wept. Victor hobbled toward him, and stroked his head.

"There's a faster way to fly, my boy," he said. "Much faster. Sleep now. I'll take you to a special place at dusk. You'll have to be brave, but you'll be home soon, I promise."

Sam was so tired, and his throat was so sore. He wasn't sure if the old bat had lost his mind like Renny had. Maybe he'd been attacked by the Gas Man too.

Victor pushed some of his straw toward Sam. "This will keep you warm. The stone is so cold.

Here. Sleep here, and we'll get you on your way home, tomorrow."

Sam sighed and closed his eyes, longing for the desert air. He wondered if he would ever feel it beneath his wings again, lifting him into the night.

Chapter 7
Sam in the Land of the Giants

At dusk, Sam was shaken awake by Victor's clawed foot. "Come! Let's go! I have a wonderful surprise!"

Sam yawned. His throat felt as if it was filled with hot sand. He tried to speak, but what came out of his mouth sounded like a toad's croak.

Victor prodded him to his feet and started pushing him toward the crack in the wall, chirping, "Come on! No time to waste! We must fly!"

Both bats reached the ledge and launched themselves into the air. Sam was struck by how graceful the old bat was in flight. From even a slight distance, you couldn't tell that he was any older than Sam.

"Where are we going?" Sam barely squeaked.

"I don't know! We're following you!" cried a familiar voice. Giorgio swooped down and raced past him. Just behind Giorgio, wing to wing, Peter, Sylvie, Aurore, Pierre, Sebastian and Coco soared, snapping up any insects unfortunate enough to cross their paths.

They all tailed the old bat, trusting that he knew where he was going. They all heard the roar seconds before a great blast of wind sent them tumbling through the air like feathers caught in a hurricane.

"WHAT WAS THAT?" Giorgio screamed, terrified. The bats, struggling to right themselves, lost sight of Victor.

"PLANE!" screamed Coco.

"WHY ARE WE FLYING TOWARDS THE PLANES?"

"Stop yelling, Giorgio." Peter had spotted Victor, who was circling back toward them. "It's gone now."

"Come!" Victor was laughing. "Let's get Sam home!"

The colony dove in unison toward the tarmac, lighting down on a sawhorse decorated with a blinking yellow light. Victor craned around the others. "Sam! Welcome to the airport!"

"Why are we here?" Sam's voice was still scratchy from all the yelling.

"Can't hear you, son."

"HE WANTS TO KNOW WHY WE'VE COME TO GET OURSELVES KILLED BY A PLANE!" Giorgio translated.

"Nonsense," Victor snapped. "No one is getting killed. Sam needs to get home. It will take him a lifetime to get back to his desert on his own, so we're going put him on a plane. They fly faster and longer than any bat ever could."

Now, finally, Sam understood. He had seen planes flying overhead in the night, heard their deafening roars. But until this moment, it had never occurred to him that they were for traveling, like the train, a car, or the ship. It never even occurred to him that people were inside them, soaring through the air like bats.

Victor pointed. "See that plane there, Sam? The one with the big hole in its belly?"

Sam saw the luggage cart, and knew exactly what the old bat meant for him to do. But he remembered the train—it had taken him away from Chelsea, not towards it.

"How do I know if the plane will take me where I need to go? What if it isn't going to land in my desert?

"Still can't hear you, son," Victor said.

"HE THINKS YOU'VE GONE CRAZY!" hollered Giorgio.

Victor turned toward Sam. "This will get you closer to home. The great big planes travel far, and fast. When you land, pop on out and sniff the air. Look at the stars. Keep your eye on the skies, and you'll know if you're close to home. If not, find another plane! It couldn't take more than a couple of tries, how many planes can there be in all the world?"

"Don't do it, Sam," Coco pleaded. "There could be millions of planes in the world, and you could travel forever, and always be lost."

"I'm lost now," Sam whispered. "He's right. Planes travel so far, and so fast, and I've traveled so far, for so long. I want to rest for a bit, and see how far this plane can take me."

"He's gone crazy, too!" Giorgio whispered.

Sam smiled, and Victor gave him a crooked smile right back. Sam turned to Coco. "Will you visit the old bat, and make sure he isn't lonely?"

"Of course I will. Of course."

With that, Sam took off for the luggage cart. He found himself a cozy pocket in a duffle bag, and waited to be loaded onto the plane.

"GOODBYE CRAZY SAM!" Giorgio yelled.

"Come along, old bat," Peter told Victor. "I'll take you home."

"I can't hear you, son."

"HE SAID HE'S TRYING TO IMPRESS COCO BY GETTING YOU HOME SAFELY!"

Peter slapped Giorgio down off the sawhorse, but Giorgio was laughing so hard, he hardly felt the sting. The colony lifted off, toward the cathedral. Only Coco looked back. blowing a kiss toward Sam. "Goodbye Sam, *petit* traveler."

Sam didn't have to wait long before two men in heavy orange jackets appeared, and began tossing the luggage into the plane's belly. Sam's duffle bag tumbled inside. He listened as the other bags and suitcases thudded into the compartment. Eventually, the door slammed shut, and the tiny room vibrated with the start of the engines.

Sam let out a squeak and burrowed further down into the pocket to drown out the noise. He hoped that when the cargo doors opened again, he'd find himself under the desert moon.

It took a full twenty-four hours with a stop to refuel in Dubai for Sam's plane to reach its destination.

Sam wasted no time. He was starving, tired, and too hot in his pocket-hiding place. The moment the doors opened, he burst from the plane's belly into fresh air... and sunlight. His belly and his brain told him it should be nighttime, but here was only bright sunny morning, with nowhere to hide.

Disoriented and hungry, Sam fluttered aimlessly. He caught the scent of ocean, animals, oil, and gasoline fumes.

Sam could see a lush, green park below, filled with trees and the sounds of birds singing. Something about it reminded him of the jungle in Argentina. He zoomed down and found a fragrant branch to rest on, while he caught his breath.

"I can hide here until the sun goes down, eat until my belly is about to burst, and hop on another plane," Sam thought aloud.

"Excellent plan, mate."

Sam looked up, and a face peered down. It was a fuzzy gray bear, with big fluffy ears and a big black nose, crunching leaves between his teeth.

The bear sat back on his branch and held his leaves close. "You can't have any, it's my tree."

"I don't want any. I don't eat leaves."

The bear relaxed "Then you're welcome to keep hanging there, like a bat."

"I am a bat," Sam said, indignant.

"You're too small to be a bat. You're just a little mouse with wings."

"I am NOT a mouse!" Sam cried, incredulous.

The bear shrugged. "Don't be offended, mate. I wish I had wings. I've just never seen such a tiny bat. Bats are more like dogs with wings."

Sam was convinced the bear had gone mad. Obviously, there was no point in arguing with someone who had lost his mind. Still, the bear lived here and might be able to answer some questions. "Have you seen any moths come by? I'm awfully hungry."

"I've seen a few butterflies. Mostly just these terrible gnats biting at my ears," the bear said, clawing the air around his head.

"Ooooh, gnats! May I have them?"

"You want to eat gnats?" The bear sounded surprised. "Wouldn't you rather eat a mango?"

Sam had no idea what a mango was. "No, I'd definitely like to have some gnats."

"Have at it, then. Just don't bite me," the bear warned.

Sam flew up to the bear. Perching on his head, Sam snapped up all the gnats he could catch. They weren't much more filling than eating breadcrumbs off a plate, but the snack took some of the painful rumbling out of Sam's belly.

"Still hungry, are you? I'm always hungry. I think I could eat this whole tree and still be hungry," yawned the pudgy bear. "You know, if you want more gnats, you should go see the elephants.

They're LOADED with them."

Sam didn't know what an elephant was, or if it was anything like a mango. But his belly was still whining. If he could catch a few more clouds of gnats, he thought, they might keep him going until sunset, when he could fly and hunt.

"Where do I find these elephants?"

The bear pointed south. "I think, maybe they're that way! Or -" he pointed west, "they could be that way. Just fly up, mate. You can't miss 'em. They're the size of a truck. Bigger. A truck on top of a truck."

Sam raised his brows in disbelief. "I'll figure it out. Thank you for the gnats."

Sam launched himself into the air, staying close to the trees. He squinted at the noon sun, fluttering in the heat. He didn't see anything as big as a truck moving below. He was so hot, he wondered if he was going to roast.

Sam settled down on the wire of a steel mesh cage just below a treetop to rest for a minute. And then the claws came toward him.

They were like rounded black hooks, charging at

him through the mesh, making a terrible racket. Sam leapt up in terror, looked down, and saw— well, what he saw between the hooks looked like bat feet. HUGE bat feet. They looked just like his, but the distance from toe to the first knuckle was longer than his whole body.

A deep voice came up from the darkness below. "HALLOOOO up there! Halllooo, little mouse!"

"Who are you talking to?" The second voice was louder, and even deeper.

And then Sam saw the second pair of hooks clawing toward him, even larger, followed by bat feet so huge he though that these must be the elephants the bear had told him about.

"Are you an elephant?" Sam called down, swooping closer... but not too close to the mesh.

"Of course I'm not an elephant! I am a bat!" the voice replied from the darkness.

If Sam had heard about what curiosity had done to the cat, he might not have done what he did next. Throwing caution to the wind, he dove down between the steel mesh for a closer look.

Inside the cage, looking back at Sam with

friendly curiosity, were half a dozen bats as big as dogs. As big as BIG dogs.

They had wild orange fur and eyes as large as silver-dollar pancakes. Their faces were dark gray, and tucked into their wings while they slept—all but two, who stared right through him, unblinking.

"Look, mummy! It's a mouse with wings!" the smaller bat squealed.

"My goodness, you're right!" The much, much larger bat sounded surprised. "It IS a flying mouse."

"I'm not a mouse!" Sam cried out. "I am a bat!"

"You're the smallest bat I've ever seen," replied the much too large bat.

Sam wondered how large the moths were that fed these bats, and worried that perhaps a moth that large would just as likely eat him. But then, the smaller bat reached out with the hook at the end of her wing and pierced a piece of fruit, hanging from a branch inside the cage.

"Would you like something to eat, tiny bat?"

Sam considered the fruit. It oozed sickly sweet-smelling nectar from the place where the bat had stabbed it. He didn't want to be rude, but it just didn't seem too appetizing.

"Thank you very much for the offer, but I prefer moths... or maybe some gnats. Or midges. Any sort of bug will do, I'm just so hungry," he pleaded.

The bats recoiled and grimaced.

"Bugs are nasty things that eat our fruit. What sort of bat eats bugs?" the too large bat asked.

"Well, if I ate the bugs, there wouldn't be any to steal your fruit," Sam countered.

The bats looked at each other. "He made a good point, Mummy!"

Sam smiled. It was obvious that, even though this bat was ridiculously large, she was still just baby. A VERY LARGE baby.

"What's your name?" Sam asked the larger of the big bats.

"Ah. Introductions. I forgot my manners," she replied. "My name is Bev, and this is my daughter, Ashley."

Ashley reached out a hook to touch Sam, and he tensed all of his muscles, fearing she would pierce him like the fruit.

"Hallo," Ashley said, and gingerly stroked Sam's wings.

"My name is Sam. It's very nice to meet you."

Sam watched as flies buzzed around the drooling wound in the fruit and released himself from his roost on the wire. He zipped back and forth through the cage, snapping up all the flies as they settled in the sticky nectar.

Ashley laughed and cheered as Sam ate up all the pests, filling his empty belly. When he was done, he flipped himself back up, rocking back and forth in the breeze that blew through the cage.

"What sort of cave is this?" Sam asked.

"It's not a cave, it's a cage," replied Bev. "Some

of the bats lived in trees, and one day they fell asleep, and woke up here. I was born here in this park. People take care of us, and come to look at us through the wire."

She pointed her hook toward a path just outside the cage, where people were in fact strolling by, pointing at them, and smiling.

The bats shared stories until late afternoon. Sam explained how he had gotten to the cage, where he was going, and how he planned to get home. The bats were fascinated by his tale, and before he was done telling it, he realized that the other bats had come closer, listening to his adventures.

When he was finished, Bev stretched her wings and then fanned herself with them. Sam's jaw dropped. Her wings were at least five feet across, and he wondered at how magnificent she would look in flight.

Sam remembered Victor and the marble, and wondered where he was on the earth.

"Bev, where am I?"

She laughed softly. "You're in the Taronga Zoo. Welcome to Australia, friend."

Sam had landed at the bottom of the world, where the stars were upside-down and the sky was filled with giants.

"That was such a lovely story, Sam," Ashley yawned. "It's made me want to nap and dream about flying in an airplane, way above the clouds. I bet you could catch the moon up there."

Bev was yawning along with her daughter. "Ashley is right, Sam. It is time for a nap. You should get some sleep before you catch another plane."

Although Sam had grown quite a bit since the earthquake had destroyed his colony's cave, he was still comforted by the mothering.

"Come. You can nap with me," Ashley offered, and stretched out her wings so Sam could cuddle inside them, like a doll. Bev gathered Ashley inside her wings as well, and the three bats snuggled together.

Sam was exhausted by the long trip, but the clock in his mind that told him it was time to sleep or wake felt broken. It was late afternoon, but Sam could have sworn it was the middle of the night, if there hadn't been a blue sky above to contradict him.

Sam's thoughts were muddled, and he barely noticed the two figures emerging from the leaves until they were upon them. He was startled into a squeak, and burrowed deeper into Ashley's wings, leaving just enough room to peek at the newcomers. They were a man and a woman, their ruddy faces etched in permanent smiles dried in place by too much sun. They wore khaki shorts and button-down shirts with rolled-up sleeves. Sam saw that they were carrying trays full of fruit, mangoes, figs, leaves, and dishes of fresh water.

The two people set the food out for the bats, whispering to each other in that odd, human language of slurry grunts and fluttering laughter.

The woman pointed toward Ashley and Bev, gently rocking in the breeze, sound asleep.

"This pair, here. These are the ones going to America," the woman said. "The vet gave them the go-ahead for the flight, and they brought in the supplies this morning."

"They won't be too happy about it, I'm guessing," said the man, reaching behind him for what appeared to be a large birdcage, which had been hidden by the plants.

"Hold still, sweet girl," whispered the woman, and stuck Bev in the bottom with a needle.

Sam froze as the woman turned to give Ashley a jab, as well. The giant bats were sleeping so deeply that neither of them flinched at all as the zookeepers gingerly unhooked their clawed feet from the mesh and placed the bats inside the cage. Sam, hidden away from their view, tucked deeper into Ashley's wings.

Then they were in motion. Sam had the sensation of being on the baggage cart in the train station. Muffled sounds made their way through the soft leathery webbing of Ashley's wings: Birds calling to each other in squawks and songs, and the bone-chilling roars of animals Sam couldn't imagine, but assumed were elephants.

The trio was transferred to a vehicle that jostled them about in a way that reminded Sam of the man's car and the trip to the Isle of Wight. It was cool and dark, and Sam closed his eyes, listening to

Ashley's breathing, slower than it had been before she was jabbed with the needle. Despite the excitement, Sam dozed. He was completely spent from his travels, and felt his body shutting down as if it were dawn.

Sam realized he was on a plane when was awakened by the vibrations of an engine. He was soaked with sweat, and struggled to get some air outside of Ashley's wings.

"I don't want to do this anymore. I want to be home," Sam whispered to Ashley. She couldn't hear him, and Sam knew that, but saying the words aloud made him feel better.

"Have I ever told you about the desert sky?" Sam knew he hadn't told her, but that didn't matter. He could feel his muscles relax as he spoke. It was like talking to the old man in the car on the way to hospital. They couldn't understand each other, but it felt good to get his thoughts in order.

He told her about the desert sky, and trying to reach the place where the earth meets the sky at dusk, just when the last bit of fiery orange sun dipped below the horizon. He described what it was like to fly out into the night air and meet a cloud of fluttering moths with his family stretched out for miles, singing and laughing in between gulps of a delicious dinner on the wind. He spoke to the sleeping Ashley until his voice gave out and he could only wonder when his next meal would come.

"I need to get home," Sam croaked, before his eyes snapped shut once more.

When the plane touched down, the dose of medicine Ashley had been given was wearing off. She began to stir, fitfully.

Her movements woke Sam. He listened as the plane came to a stop, and human feet shuffled across the floor. He heard doors opening, people's voices speaking and laughing. The cage jerked and shook. They were on the move, once again, and Ashley was twitching.

"Ashley! Ashley! Please wake up!" Sam pleaded, but though Ashley yawned and twisted, she did not answer.

They were wheeled out, and loaded onto something. A truck? He heard the engine start and felt vibrations. It felt like hours had gone by before they were again unloaded, wheeled about, jostled some more, and then set down.

Sam wriggled and cried out, trying to wake his snoozing captors. Just when he had convinced himself that he'd never get free, Ashley stretched her wings, and Sam tumbled out. Finally free, he fell like a stone onto the floor of the cage, gasping for air.

"What's this?"

The zookeeper reached down and picked Sam up in her gloved hands. She was gentle, cupping her hands slightly, but keeping Sam still with his wings between her fingers. She peered down at him.

"How on earth....?"

The zookeeper's mouth dropped into an O of disbelief. How had a Mexican Freetail bat gotten all the way to Australia, and hitched a ride back to the southwest's San Diego Zoo, inside the wings of a baby Flying Fox bat? So far as the zookeeper was aware, there weren't any Freetails housed at the Taronga zoo, where Ashley and Bev had come from.

She gingerly placed Sam in a little packing box, and shut the lid. "Don't worry, little guy. We'll get you back out into the world."

Sam didn't understand what she was saying, but recognized the kindness in her voice. He wasn't frightened when she set Sam and his box on the passenger seat of a car. The zookeeper was headed home, after settling the zoo's new flying foxes in their habitat.

Just a few miles from the Mexican border, she pulled her car over to the side of the freeway. It was dusk, just that time when the sun was sinking below the horizon, and the desert sky was a water-color painting of orange, purple, and an ever-deeper blue.

"Here you go, little traveler." She got out of the car, with Sam's box in hand. "Fly away home."

Taking the lid off, she shook the box gently and set Sam free, back into the American Southwest.

Chapter 8
Home is Wherever She Is

With the night breeze moving under his wings, Sam took off, soaring higher and higher up toward the desert moon. He sang loud and strong, listening for the echoes of beating wings. He heard them right away—and they were close.

He zoomed across the sky. Minutes later, he caught the first of the hundred moths he would crunch that night. It was perfect. Fluffy, powdery, crispy goodness filled his cheeks, and then his belly. As he flew higher and faster into the desert, he looked up and saw the stars, twinkling bright and fierce against the black velvet sky. Away from the freeway, deeper and deeper into land where there were no people, Sam listened to the echoes of the desert bouncing back to his ears every time he called out. Tears of joy streaked his face and evaporated as he flew into the wind.

This was home. He wished that Victor could see these stars and this moon. And he supposed he would, when the earth turned away from the sun. But in Paris, it was the city that twinkled spectacularly below, and Sam thought that the old bat should see what stars really looked like when there was nothing to dull them.

He thought of his mother, of Bonnie, and most of all, of his ancestors. He wondered how many of them had crisscrossed this land before settling in the cave where he was born. His heart pounded and he closed his eyes as he beat his wings against a cross wind that lifted him up so high he could almost touch the moon with the tip of his wing.

Sam flew east, following the moths as they migrated from Mexico. He kept a careful eye on the stars and moon, and counted one half moon and a full since his release from the zookeeper's box. He was going to head back towards the west once he reached the second full moon, so he'd not stray too far from the precious desert.

In the daytime, he roosted in trees or old barns. At night, he outflew the owls and hawks who hunted him. He was content, at peace, and had all but forgotten about his search for the bridge, sure that it was only a story, no more real than a bat who could be so ugly as to turn another bat to stone.

As the moon got larger, he saw that he was getting closer to city lights. The stars were slightly dimmer, and the smell of gasoline fumes wafted toward him on the wind.

Just outside of a city that people called Austin, Texas, Sam stopped to roost in the knotty hole of a dying tree, checking it as a possible hiding place for when the sun rose. As he was deciding the tree would work, he heard something that made him freeze right where he was: the familiar clicks and chirps of bats like him echoing off rocks and trees. And they were nearby.

Was it possible? More than two years had passed since the earthquake, and Sam hadn't seen or heard another bat like himself since then. Craning his neck and watching the skies from his roost, Sam saw fluttering wings overhead. He couldn't quite move, but felt his heart thundering in his chest.

"Maybe," Sam said to himself. "Maybe there is a bridge, after all."

The sky was beginning to brighten, and Sam watched the bats fly eastward. He knew that they were headed home after the hunt, and he resolved to wait for them to return, to fly up and hunt with them, to listen to their hunting songs and feel their chatter bounce off his ears.

Sam woke early that evening, feeling as if he hadn't really slept at all. He shot out of the knotty hole like a bullet, ignoring his surroundings in his eagerness to meet the colony. The lack of sleep dampened his senses—aiming for a moth, he veered full speed into a pinecone. The impact knocked him out of the air, sending him tumbling through the dirt and landing bottom-end-up in a cloud of dust.

Laughter filled the air from all directions. It was the clumsiest, most ridiculous looking stunt, and Sam realized he had done it directly in sight of the colony he wanted so badly to join.

"Are you all right?" The small, clear voice came from behind him, a voice as sweet and crisp as a candy apple.

Sam dusted himself off as best he could. "I think so," he stammered, "Um. So. That was embarrassing. I didn't really sleep well. I'm not usually this clumsy."

Perched on the ground beside him was a free-tail bat. Her fur was a dusky gray that reminded him of what the sun had looked like, rising through the fog on the Isle of Wight. Her eyes were ringed in black, and her snout had a slight curve that pointed downward to a gentle smile.

"It's okay. Let me help you up." She offered her other wing as a balance. "Come, let's hunt, and I'll keep you safe from those horrible pine cones."

She smiled, and suddenly Sam wasn't quite so tired anymore.

"Thank you," he told her.

He tried to think of the right combination of words that would make her see him as anything other than a fool, but everything that came to mind sounded awkward or strange. Instead, he concentrated on hunting and avoiding any other clumsy mistakes that might make her think he was as ridiculous as he felt.

They flew side by side, a wing's length apart, swirling through the air and chomping down on the moths and mosquitoes that buzzed across their path.

She didn't speak again, and neither did he. They simply hunted, as bats do at night, and have done since bats first had wings. As the sky turned from black to blue, she made a wide turn in the sky and flashed her smile once again.

"I'm glad you're all right. Maybe I'll see you again?" And then she was off.

Her question went unanswered as Sam again searched for words that wouldn't come. He didn't follow her—she hadn't invited him to do so. He watched her fly up over the trees toward a river that glowed orange with the sun. It made her look like a spark from a flame, floating through the air.

Sam found a thick pine to roost in for the day, camouflaged behind prickly bunches of dry needles. Some poked into his sides, but he couldn't even feel them. He was struck happily numb with love. He was going to find her, he thought, and find the perfect set of words to string together. And then he was going to spend the rest of his days hunting wing-to-wing with this lovely bat...

"ARGH!" He smacked himself with a wing. "I didn't even ask her NAME!"

Sam stayed in the pine tree long after he woke that evening, practicing introductions in his mind, clearing his throat, stretching his wings. He was nervous in a way he had never been in his life. It wasn't fear, exactly, but a longing for something so dear and precious and fragile that he was afraid that the wrong word or a careless glance might break it like a robin's egg. This was the terrible wonderful pain of love.

He was so preoccupied with practicing making a good impression on her, he didn't notice that the roost had begun the hunt. The sky was flowing with bats.

Sam groomed himself one last time and took flight. For once, he wasn't keeping a sharp eye on dinner. Instead, he was looking for the enchanting stranger who had helped him up. He had almost flown right past her when he heard that candy apple voice.

"I thought you might come back to teach that pinecone a lesson."

And there she was, perched above the cone that had knocked him from the air the night before. Sam laughed, made a wide turn, and perched beside her.

"I'm Sam."

It was simple, and not at all like the poetry he had written and rewritten a thousand times in his mind that dusk. She smiled at him.

"I'm Nina."

She was the deep, endless beauty of Bonnie's eyes, the mischievous grin on Jilli's face, the kindness of Victor, the coolness of Coco, and the gentle comfort of the mother ship rat multiplied by one million squared. That was Nina. And here she was, choosing to perch on this pine branch, under these stars, with Sam. He wondered what he had done to deserve her company. Out of the millions of bats filling the sky, Sam and Nina could only see each other.

Nina wanted to hear the stories that had forged Sam's smile of open kindness. He was happy to share them with her. He told her about every embarrassing blunder and heroic gesture that occurred during his journey, he told her about Jilli, Tomas, Renny, Victor, and the giant bats of Australia, and Nina listened, fascinated.

Then it was Nina's turn to share stories of her home, family, and life.

"A very long time ago, my ancestors lived inside a cave in the desert, a lot like yours. They spent their days inside, telling stories and napping in the dark. When they burst out of the cave to hunt, the desert horizon would glow orange and purple, and then they would meet the great swarm of moths and eat until their bellies were round and full."

She paused to snap up a bit more dinner, but Sam was hanging on her every word, as she described the cave.

"But then there was a terrible drought, and the great swarm became a small flutter, and everyone was going hungry. To save the colony, my family left the dark cave and traveled for a long time over the land, battling owls and hunger all the way. Many were lost on the journey. And then they came upon the river, and a feast of moths met them in the sky. They ate late into the night, and as the sun came up, they found shelter under a bridge on the river, and that's where they stayed. When my mama told me that our colony had lived in a cave, I couldn't imagine it, living indoors without the sound of the river rushing underneath us. I don't think I could fall asleep without that lovely sound. It's like a lullaby. When we wake to hunt, people standing on the bridge cheer and clap for our colony. Chelsea sounds lovely, Sam, but I think my bridge is the best place in all the world to be a bat."

Sam felt his body become weightless, the only thing keeping him aloft was the wind and his open wings. All of his senses were focused on Nina's words, and what they meant.

"I think," Sam stammered. "I think maybe your family came from my cave, Nina. My mama told me that our colony had been living in our cave---"

"Ever since bats had wings," Nina finished.

"And she told me about the drought, and the river..."

Neither of them spoke for a long time. They flew wing-to-wing, forgetting the moths and not hearing the other bats in the sky calling to each other.

"Sam, did you ever hear a story about a bat named Ricardo who escaped an owl by steering a swarm of locusts into his path?"

"He was my great-great-great grampa!" Sam puffed with pride.

They talked throughout the night, ignoring hunger and the approaching dawn, sharing their common history. Sam found himself shooing moths away instead of eating them. He didn't want to miss a word Nina said. When she laughed, it was always full and open and bold.

Sam loved her, and knew that his home was wherever she was. Deep in his heart, he knew she felt the same. He just knew, the same way he knew when it was time to sleep, and time to hunt. It was time to be in love.

"It's getting late, Sam. We should head home."

Eventually, the river came into view, and the Congress Avenue bridge stretching over it in silhouette against the Austin dawn. Sam thought it was more majestic than Tower Bridge, and more beautiful than the Seine in Paris. He found himself agreeing with Nina. This was the best place in all the world to be a bat.

The horizon brightened into a brilliant orange and the last of the stars were chased away by the dawn. Sam and Nina flew toward the bridge in silence, content in each other's company. The pair found a comfy spot to roost until nightfall. With the gentle sound of water moving below them, they quickly fell asleep.

Sam snuggled against her, nuzzling her cheek. That night, when he dreamed, he dreamt of family.

162

CPSIA information can be obtained
at www.ICGtesting.com
Printed in the USA
LVHW040314070520
655160LV00002B/366